Antigone

Adapted by
Lewis Galantiere

from the play by
Jean Anouilh

A Samuel French Acting Edition

SAMUEL FRENCH
FOUNDED 1830
New York Hollywood London Toronto
SAMUELFRENCH.COM

ISBN   978-0-573-60546-8   Printed   in   U.S.A.   #35

IMPORTANT BILLING AND CREDIT REQUIREMENTS

Copy of program of the first performance of ANTIGONE
as produced at the Cort Theatre, New York,
February 19, 1946.

KATHARINE CORNELL

In Association with Gilbert Miller presents

ANTIGONE

Adapted by Lewis Galantiere

From the play by Jean Anouilh

with

CEDRIC HARDWICKE

Bertha Belmore	Horace Braham
Ruth Matteson	Wesley Addy
George Mathews	and Miss Cornell

Staged by Guthrie McClintic

Setting by Raymond Sovey

Costumes by Valentina

CHORUS .... *Horace Braham*
ANTIGONE .... *Katharine Cornell*
NURSE .... *Bertha Belmore*
ISMENE .... *Ruth Matteson* sister
HAEMON .... *Wesley Addy* son
CREON .... *Cedric Hardwicke* King
FIRST GUARD .... *George Mathews*
SECOND GUARD .... *David J. Stewart*
THIRD GUARD .... *Michael Higgins*
MESSENGER .... *Oliver Cliff*
PAGE .... *Alfred Biondo* attendant
EURYDICE .... *Merle Maddern* queen

5

ANTIGONE

A Note By The Adapter

When Sophocles was writing his tragedies, 2,400 years ago, the Greeks were already telling of a girl named Antigone who was said to have lived in the city of Thebes in a mythical past. Her father was King Oedipus, and a kind of Greek Job. Her mother was Queen Jocasta, who had married Oepidus following the mysterious killing of her first husband, Laius. Antigone had a sister name Ismene, as well as two brothers, Eteocles and Polynices. The boys were older than the girls; but which boy was the elder, and which girl, nobody could say with assurance even in Sophocles' time. There was also an uncle named Creon, who was Jocasta's brother.

Sophocles told the story of this doomed and princely family in three parts, of which his "Antigone," as well as ours, deals only with the last. The first part reveals that Oedipus, unknown to himself, had committed two particularly repellent sins. Brought up from infancy at a foreign court, he had returned as a man to Thebes, had killed his own father, Laius, and had married his own mother, Jocasta, by whom he had the four children already named. This horror made known, Jocasta hangs herself, and Oedipus, after putting out his own eyes, takes the child Antigone begging with him on the highways of Hellas. The second part treats of a period in which Oedipus is about to die in exile and Antigone will return to Thebes. Oedipus has been deposed, and it has been agreed that his sons shall share their father's throne, each to reign over Thebes in alternate years. The sons have incurred their father's wrath and he has laid upon them a curse that they shall die by one another's hand. When Eteocles has reigned a full year, he refuses to yield up the throne to his brother. The two princes go to war—Eteocles at the head of a Theban army and Plynices as the beseiger of Thebes, supported by six foreign princes. The foreigners are defeated and the curse is fulfilled: Polynices and Eteocles kill one another in single combat just outside the seven-gated city. Creon, their uncle, becomes king of Thebes.

It is at this point that "Antigone" opens. The "plot" of the play is simple. Creon has ordained that Eteocles shall be buried with honors while the corpse of Polynices is to be left to be mangled by the vultures and the dogs. Anyone who attempts to give Polynices burial is himself to be put to death. Antigone, revolted by this godless and inhuman edict, tries to bury her brother. She is caught. And as is always the case with martyrs, her revolt bears fruit only after her death.

It is interesting, I think, that Sophocles' own "Antigone" is already an "adaptation" of the original tale in the fact that he virtually makes Athenians of his principal Thebans. Like ourselves, the people of Athens had a deep sense of the sanctity of human personality, a profound belief that all men—friends and enemies, the righteous and the unrighteous—were created by God, possessed some sort of immortality, and deserved sacramental burial. The Thebans, on the other hand, were a barbarian tribe who left the enemy dead to rot. (Indeed, Euripides wrote a play, "The Suppliants," in which Theseus, the King of Athens, who was Opedius' protector during his exile, actually makes war upon the Thebans in order to force them to bury their enemy dead.) Yet Sophocles does not permit Creon to argue like a logical Theban, but makes him argue like a criminal Athenian. He does not permit him to say that Theban law and Theban religion do not require him to bury his enemies but makes him concentrate, as if he were an atheist-dictator of Athens, upon the political aspect of his situation. "Is not the State the property of the ruler?" Creon is made to ask. "Shall the people dictate what I ordain?" It is this political injustice against which Creon's son, Haemon, protests. It is this dictatorship that frightens the half-protesting Elders of Thebes.

Antigone, on the other hand, is concerned with an outrage against the body of her brother, and not with politics. The outrage swells and grows in her mind's eye until she sees it as an offense against God and against all men. And before she does, Sophocles makes her say, "By a deed of piety, I have won the reward of impiety." Her protest and her martyrdom have the effect of a revelation to the Thebans. All of this might occur in any country where a dictator sets himself above both religion and the people.

Nothing could exceed the ingenuity of M. Jean Anouilh's treatment of this subject in a text which, written and produced in Paris in 1943, had to receive the sanction of a German censor before it could be performed in the presence of the German State Police. He made of his Antigone a martyr who refused to say yes (literally and figuratively), not only to the desecration of Polynices but even more to the kind of life that Creon offered her—a life in which she is promised "happiness" provided that she will agree not to intervene in anything that does not concern her material existence. Under the stress and the indignity of the Occupation, M. Anouilh's Antigone was able to symbolize for all Frenchmen, France herself, France rejecting the German "New Order" with its promise of prosperity, of "happiness," provided the French people would agree to surrender their spiritual independence —which is to say, their souls.

The character of Creon offered a more difficult problem. On the one hand, M. Anouilh had to content the Germans in his portrayal of a ruler. On the other hand, he had his compatriots to think of. The central difficulty was that, in the matter of Polynices, Creon's case was founded upon a moral equivalent of political purges, Matteotti murders, and lynchings. We can hardly imagine a Lincoln or a Franklin Roosevelt taking the unburied body of an enemy as the point of departure of a political program. M. Anouilh managed, however, to put into Creon's mouth words which satisfied the Germans while permitting patriotic Frenchmen to interpret them as a call to place the general interest higher than their separate private interests. It is hard to find an American analogy, but we may say that for Frenchmen, the play might almost have been one about Abe Lincoln and the sister of a Confederate spy.

The reader will have to take my word for it that only a citizen of a German-occupied country (or, by analogy, a Southerner of 1863) would be able to come away from M. Anouilh's play with the feeling that Antigone's case was stronger than Creon's. For I should be less than frank if I did not say that the play in which Miss Cornell and Sir Cedric Hardwicke will open at the Cort Theatre tomorrow night is not in every respect the play which M. Anouilh gave to Occupied France in 1943.

This is not to say that the force of Creon's arguments has been diminished. Those who hear them will, I believe, still find that Creon is perhaps one of the most persuasive dictators ever portrayed on the stage. The lines are still M. Anouilh's—conveyed in such English as I was able to find for his masterly eloquence. It was important that we should hear his arguments, I thought. But it was equally important to indicate that those arguments have no validity against a higher law which assumes the existence of an immortal soul and commands that priest or rabbi or pastor shall accompany a man to the electric chair as readily as to the field of battle.

This has been done, not by taking anything away from M. Anouilh's Creon, but by adding something to his Antigone, his Chorus, and his Haemon.

A final word. It will be asked, perhaps, "Why rewrite Sophocles?" For one thing, this story never belonged exclusively to Sophocles. Euripides (who was his contemporary for seventy-four years) was only one of those who have told the story quite differently.

For another, each age is entitled to its own Antigone, quite as every country is entitled to its own Faustus. We have already seen that M. Anouilh had a special reason for his version. But the best retort is perhaps to be found in these words of the great Dryden: "Whenever I have liked any story in a romance, novel or foreign play, I have made no difficulty, nor ever shall, to take the foundation of it, to build it up, and to make it proper for the English stage .... The story is the least part .... The forming it into acts and scenes, disposing of acts and passions in their proper places, and beautifying both with descriptions, similitudes, and proprieties of language, is the principal employment of the poet."

I believe there is no assailing this argument—except, of course, by demonstrating in any particular instance that the result was not worth the effort.

—LEWIS GALANTIERE.

ANTIGONE

THE CAST
(In the order in which they speak)

CHORUS
ANTIGONE
NURSE
ISMENE
HAEMON
CREON
FIRST GUARD
SECOND GUARD
THIRD GUARD
MESSENGER
PAGE
EURYDICE

THE SETTING

A gray cloth cyclorama, semi-circular, hangs at the back of the set. The cyclorama has a vent in the Center for entrance and exit. At the bottom of the cyclorama, a stair, of three steps, sweeps in a semicircle. Downstage Right and Left, two archways.

A table stands Left of Center stage, with matching chairs set at either end. A small stool is placed by the Right side of the chair at the Right end of the table.

ANTIGONE

ANTIGONE, *her hands clasped round her left knee and staring straight ahead, sits on the top step, Right Center. The* THREE GUARDS *sit on the steps Center in a small group, playing a game of cards. The* CHORUS *stands up Left Center, on the top step.* EURYDICE *sits on the top step, just Left of Center, knitting. The* NURSE *sits on the second step, Left of* EURYDICE. ISMENE *stands in front of arch Left, facing toward* HAEMON, *who stands Left of her.* CREON *sits in the chair at Right end of the table. His* PAGE *stands behind* CREON. *The* MESSENGER *is leaning against the downstage portal of the Right arch.*

The Curtain rises slowly; then the CHORUS *turns and moves down to below the Left end of table.*

CHORUS. Well, here we are. These people that you see here are about to act out for you the story of Antigone. *(He looks at* ANTIGONE*)* That dark-haired girl sitting by herself, staring straight ahead, seeing nothing, is Antigone. She is thinking. She is thinking that the instant I finish telling you who's who and what's what in this play, she will burst forth as the dark, tense, serious girl, who is about to rise up and face the whole world alone—alone against the world and against Creon, her uncle, the King. *(*CHORUS *moves to below chair Left of table)* Another thing that she is thinking is this: she is going to die. Antigone is young. She would much rather live than die. But there is no help for it. When you are on the side of the gods

13

against the tyrant, of Man against the State, of purity against corruption—when, in short, your name is Antigone, there is only one part you can play; (CHORUS *turns and looks at her*) and she will have to play hers through to the end. (CHORUS *returns to below Left end of table*) Mind you, Antigone doesn't know all these things about herself. I know them because it is my business to know them. That's what a Greek Chorus is for. All that she knows is that Creon won't allow her dead brother to be buried; and that despite Creon, she must bury him. Antigone doesn't *think*, she acts, she doesn't *"reason,"* she feels. And from the moment the curtain went up, she began to feel that inhuman forces were whirling her out of this world, snatching her away from her sister Ismene— (CHORUS *indicates* ISMENE) whom you see smiling at that young man; *(He turns and moves to upper Left end of table; points toward AN-TIGONE)* making *her* an instrument of the gods in a way she cannot fathom but that she will faithfully pursue. (CHORUS *looks toward audience*) You have never seen inhuman forces at work? You will, tonight. (CHORUS *moves down to below Center of table, turns and indicates* HAEMON) The young man with Ismene —with the gay and golden Ismene—is Haemon. He is the king's son, Creon's son. The apple of the tyrant's eye. Antigone and he are engaged to be married. You wouldn't have thought she was his type. He likes dancing, sports, competition: he likes women, too. (CHORUS *looks at* ISMENE) Now look at Ismene again. She is certainly more beautiful than Antigone. *She* is the girl you'd think he'd go for. (CHORUS *moves to downstage Left Center*) Well— There was a ball one night. Ismene wore a new evening dress. She was radiant. Haemon danced every dance with her: he wouldn't look at any other girl. And yet, that same night, before the dance was over, suddenly he went in search of Antigone, found her sitting alone— *(He turns and indicates* ANTIGONE) like *that*, with her arms clasped round her knees—and asked her to marry him. It didn't seem to surprise Antigone in the least. She looked up at him out of those solemn eyes of hers, then smiled sort of sadly; and she said "yes." That was all. And, well, here is Haemon expecting to marry Antigone. He won't, of course. (ANTIGONE *rises, moves to arch Right and exits.* HAEMON *watches* ANTIGONE *exit.* ISMENE *notices his glance.*) He didn't know, when he asked her, that the earth wasn't made to hold a husband of Antigone and that this princely distinction was to earn him no more than the right to die sooner than he might otherwise have done. (ISMENE *turns, goes toward arch Left and exits.* CHORUS *turns toward* CREON, *then goes up Left side of the table to above the Right end of table; stands at Left of* CREON) That grey-haired, powerfully built man sitting lost in thought with his little page at his side is Creon, the King. His face is lined. He is tired. He practices the difficult art of a leader of men. (HAEMON *starts to slowly cross, upstage, toward the arch Right, through which* ANTIGONE *has gone out, and then exits*) When he was younger, when Oedipus was King and Creon was no more than the King's brother-in-law, he was different. He loved music, bought rare manuscripts, was a kind of art patron. He used to while away whole afternoons in the antique shops of this city of Thebes. But Oedipus died. Oedipus' sons died. Creon's moment had come. He *took* over the kingdom. (CHORUS *moves down Right side of the table and then below it to Left Center. Reflects a moment*) I'll tell you something about Creon. He has a tendency to fool himself. This leader of men, this brilliant debator and logician, likes to believe that if it were *not* for his sense of responsibilty, he would step right down from the throne and go back to collecting manuscripts. But the fact is, he loves being king. He's an artist who has always believed that *he* could govern just as well as any man of action could; and he's quite sure that no god nor any man can tell *him* anything about what is best for the common people. Creon has a wife, a queen. (CHORUS *moves to front of downstage part of the Left arch*) Her name is Eurydice. *(He indicates* EURYDICE*)* There she sits, the gracious lady with the knitting, next to the old Nurse, who brought up the two girls. (CHORUS *returns to below chair Left of the table*) She will go on knitting all through the play, till the time comes for her to go to her room and die. (EURYDICE *rises, goes toward arch Right and exits*) She is a good woman, a worthy, loving soul. But she is no help to her husband. (MESSENGER *changes his stance against the Right arch*) Creon has to face the music alone. Alone with his Page, who is too young to be of any help. (NURSE *rises, goes to arch Left and exits. He looks around, then moves to upper Left end of the table*) The others? Well, let's see. (*He points toward the* MESSENGER) That pale young man leaning against the wall—that is the Messenger. Later on, he will come running in to announce that Haemon is dead. (MESSENGER *straightens up, turns, and slowly exits through Right arch*) He has a premonition of catastrophe. That's what he is brooding over. That's why he won't mingle with the others. (CHORUS *moves up to below Center of the steps and then indicates the* THREE GUARDS) As for those three pasty-faced card players —they are the guards, members of Creon's police force. They chew tobacco; one smells of garlic, another of beer; but they're not a bad lot. (GUARDS *stop playing cards, gather up the cards, rise and go toward Right arch, exit*) They have wives they are afraid of, kids who are afraid of them; they're bothered by the little day-to-day worries that beset us all. At the same time —they are policemen: eternally innocent, no matter what crimes are committed; (CREON *rises and with his* PAGE, *exits through curtain up Center. The* PAGE *holds the curtain open for* CREON, *and draws it closed as he follows* CREON *out*) eternally indifferent, for nothing that happens can matter to them. They are quite prepared to arrest anybody at all, including Creon himself, should the order be given by a *new* leader. (CHORUS *moves downstage to below the table*) That's the lot. Now for the play. (*He takes out a cigarette and lights it*) Oedipus, who was the father of the two girls, Antigone and Ismene, had also two sons, Eteocles and

Polynices. *(The LIGHTS on the stage start to gradually dim down lower)* After Oedipus died, it was agreed that the two sons should share his throne, each to reign over Thebes in alternate years. But when Eteocles, the elder son, had reigned a full year, and time had come for him to step down, he refused to yield up the throne to his younger brother, Polynices. There was civil war. Polynices brought up allies—seven foreign princes; and in the course of the war the foreigners were defeated, each in front of one of the seven gates of the city. *(CHORUS moves over to downstage Left Center)* Eteocles and Polynices met in combat and killed one another just outside the city walls—and now Creon is King. A reign of terror has begun. *(CHORUS moves over to the Left proscenium arch and leans against it. By now the stage is dark, with only the cyclorama bathed in dark blue. A single SPOT lights up the face of the* CHORUS*)* Creon has issued a solemn edict that Eteocles, on whose side he was, is to be buried with pomp and honors, and that the younger brother, Polynices, is to be left to rot. The vultures and the dogs are to bloat themselves on his carcass. And above all, any person who attempts to give him decent burial will himself be put to death. It is against this blasphemy that Antigone rebels. What is for Creon merely the climax of a political purge, is for her a hideous offense against God and Man. Since time began, men have recoiled with horror from the desecration of the dead. It is this spirit which prompts us today to suspend battle in order to bury our dead, to bury even the enemy dead.

(The LIGHT on the CHORUS *fades out quickly and the* CHORUS *exits behind the Left tormentor portal. The stage is bathed in a dark blue color. From a distance, the sound of a CLOCK striking four is heard. It is dawn, grey and ashen, in a house asleep.* ANTIGONE *steals in from out-of-doors, through the arch Right. She is carrying her sandals in her hand. She pauses down Right, looking off*

through the arch, taut, listening, then turns and moves Left across downstage. As she reaches the table she sees the NURSE *approaching through the arch Left.* ANTIGONE *quickly runs toward the exit up Center. When she reaches the steps, the* NURSE *enters through arch Left and stops Left when she sees* ANTIGONE *on the steps.)*

NURSE. *Where* have you been? (NURSE *moves across to up Left Center.)*

ANTIGONE. *(On the steps, turns toward* NURSE*)* Nowhere. It was beautiful. The whole world was grey when I went out. And now—you wouldn't recognize it. It's like a post card: all pink, and green and yellow. You'll have to get up earlier, Nurse, if you want to see a world without color.

(The LIGHTING dims up slowly to suggest the first break-of-day.)

NURSE. *(Moves up to Left and below of* ANTIGONE*)* It was still pitch black when I got up. I went to your room, for I thought you might have flung off your blanket in the night. You weren't there.

ANTIGONE. *(Comes down the steps to upstage Center)* The garden was lovely. It was still asleep.

NURSE. You hadn't slept in your bed. I couldn't find you. I went to the back door. You'd left it half open.

ANTIGONE. The fields were wet. They were waiting for something to happen. The whole world was breathless, waiting. I can't tell you what a roaring noise I seemed to make as I went up the road. *(She moves down to the stool and sits)* I took off my sandals and slipped into a field.

NURSE. *(Goes to below chair* R. *of table and kneels there)* You'll do well to wash your feet before you go back to bed, Miss.

ANTIGONE. I'm not going back to bed.

NURSE. *(Picks up* ANTIGONE's *left foot and chafes it)* Don't be a fool! You get some sleep! And *me*, getting up to see if she hasn't flung off her blanket; and I find her bed cold and nobody in it! (NURSE *puts left shoe on* ANTIGONE'S *foot.)*

ANTIGONE. Do you think that if I got up every morning like this, it would be just as thrilling *every* morning to be the first person out-of-doors?

NURSE. *Morning* my grandmother! It was night. It still is. And now, my girl, you'll stop trying to squirm out of this and tell me what you were up to. (NURSE *puts down* ANTIGONE'S *left foot)* Where've you been? (NURSE *picks up* ANTIGONE'S *right foot and chafes it.)*

ANTIGONE. That's true. It was still night. There wasn't a soul out-of-doors but me who thought that it was morning.

NURSE. *(Places right shoe on* ANTIGONE'S *foot)* Oh, my little flibbety-gibbety! Just can't imagine what I'... talking about, can she? Go on with you! I know the game. I was a girl myself once; and just as pig-headed and hard to handle as you are. *(She puts down* ANTIGONE'S *foot and then brushes off the hem of* ANTIGONE'S *skirt)* You went out to meet someone, didn't you? *Deny* it if you can.

ANTIGONE. Yes. I went out to meet someone.

NURSE. You have a lover?

ANTIGONE. Yes, Nurse. I have a lover.

NURSE. *(Stands up; bursting out)* Well, that's *very* nice now, isn't it? Such goings-on! *(The LIGHTING dims up gradually to a higher mark) You,* the daughter of a king, running out to meet lovers. And we work our fingers to the bone for you, we slave to bring you up like young ladies! *(She sits chair Right of table)* You're all alike, all of you. Even you—who never used to stop to primp in front of a looking-glass, or smear your mouth with rouge, or dindle and dandle to make the boys ogle you, and you ogle back. How many times I would say to myself, "Now that one, now: I wish she was a little more of a coquette—always wearing the same dress, her hair tumbling round her face. One thing's sure," I'd say to myself, "none of the boys will ever look at *her* while Ismene's around, all curled and cute and tidy and trim: I'll have this one on my hands the rest of my life." And now, you see? Just like your sister after all. Only worse: a hypocrite! God save us! I took her when she wasn't that high. I promised her poor mother I'd make a lady of her. And look at her! But don't you go thinking this is the end of this, my young 'un. *I'm* only your nurse and you can play deaf and dumb with me. I don't count. But you uncle Creon will hear of this! *That,* I promise you.

ANTIGONE. *(A little weary)* Yes. Creon will hear of this.

NURSE. And we'll hear what *he* has to say when he finds out that you go wandering alone o' nights. Not to mention Haemon. For the girl's engaged! Going to be married! Going to be married, and she hops out of 'ed at four in the morning to meet somebody else in a field.

ANTIGONE. Please, Nurse, I want to be alone.

NURSE. *(Quickly)* And if you so much as speak of it, she says she wants to be alone!

ANTIGONE. Nanny, don't scold. This isn't a day when you should be losing your temper.

NURSE. Not scold, indeed! Along with the rest of it, I'm to like it. Didn't I promise your mother? What would *she* say if she was here? "Old Stupid!" That's what she'd call me. "Old Stupid. Not to know how to keep my little girls pure! Spend your life making them behave, watching over them like a mother hen, and then at four o'clock in the morning snoring in your bed and letting them slip out into the night." That's what she'd say, your mother. And I'd stand there, dying of shame if I wasn't dead already. And all I could do would be not to dare look her in the face; and "That's true," I'd say, "that's all true what you say, Your Majesty." *(She dabs at her eyes with the end of her shawl.)*

ANTIGONE. *(Puts her left arm around* NURSE*)* Nanny, dear, don't cry. You'll be able to look Mamma in the face when it's your time to see her. And she'll say, "Good morning, Nanny. Thank you for my little Antigone. You did look after her so well." She knows why I went out this morning. *(She draws her arm away.)*

NURSE. *(Looks at* ANTIGONE*)* Not to meet a lover?

ANTIGNOE. No. Not to meet a lover.

NURSE. Well, you have a queer way of teasing me, I must say! (NURSE *rises, mo es away to above table)* Not to know when she's teasing me! I must be getting awfully old, that's what it is. Your sister was always the sweet-natured one; *(She returns to behind ANTIGONE)* but I too': it into my head that *you* were the one that was fondest of me. But if you really *loved* me, you'd tell me the truth. You'd tell me *why* your bed was empty when I went along to tuck you in. Wouldn't you?

ANTIGONE. Nanny, dear, don't cry. Don't cry. (ANTIGONE *turns partly upstage to face toward the* NURSE; *puts her arm around the* NURSE's *shoulder. With her other hand,* ANTIGONE *caresses* NURSE's *face)* There, now, my sweet red apple. Do you remember how I used to rub your cheeks to make them shine? My dear, wrinkled red apple! I didn't do anything tonight that was worth sending tears down the little gullies of your face. *(The LIGHTING dims up slowly to a higher mark)* I'm pure, and I swear that I have no other lover than Haemon. If you like, I'll swear that I shall never have any other lover than Haemon. Save your tears, Nanny; you may still need them. (ANTIGONE *rises, moves to upstage Right Center)* When you cry like that, I become a little girl again; and I mustn't be a little girl today.

ISMENE. (ISMENE *enters through arch Left. She pauses in front of arch)* Antigone! What are you doing, up at this hour? I've just been to your room. (ISMENE *moves to upstage Left Center.)*

NURSE. The *two* of you, now! You're both going mad, to be up before the kitchen fire has been started. (NURSE *moves to the stool, picks it up and carries it to behind the table; and places it there, away from the table somewhat)* Do you *like* running about without a mouthful of breakfast? Do you think it's decent for the daughters of a king? *(She moves a few steps toward* ISMENE*)* And look at you with no wraps on, and the sun not up! *(She turns and moves a few steps toward* ANTIGONE*)* I'll have you both on my hands with colds before I know it.

ANTIGONE. *(Moves a step to Right of* NURSE*)* Nanny, dear, go away now. It's not chilly, really: summer's here. Go get me something to eat. *(She goes a step downstage)* It would do me so much good.

NURSE. *(Goes to Left of* ANTIGONE, *places her hand on* ANTIGONE's *forehead)* My poor baby! Her head's swimming, what with nothing on her stomach, *(*NURSE *turns and crosses behind table toward arch Left)* and I stand here like an idiot when I could be getting her something hot to drink. *(*NURSE *exits through arch Left.)*

(A pause.)

ISMENE. *(Moves to above Center of table)* Aren't you well?

ANTIGONE. Yes, of course. Just a little tired. Because I got up too early. *(*ANTIGONE *goes to chair Right and sits, suddenly tired.)*

ISMENE. *(Moves to upper Right end of table)* I couldn't sleep, either.

ANTIGONE. Ismene, you ought not to go without your beauty sleep.

ISMENE. Don't make fun of me.

ANTIGONE. I'm not, truly. This particular morning, seeing how beautiful you are makes everything easier for me. Oh, wasn't I a nasty little beast when we were small? *(She takes* ISMENE's *hand in hers)* I used to fling mud at you, and put worms down your neck. I can remember tying you to a tree and cutting off your hair. Your beautiful hair! *(She rises and strokes* ISMENE's *hair)* How easy it must be never to be unreasonable with all that smooth silken hair so beautifully set around your head.

ISMENE. *(Takes* ANTIGONE's *hand in hers)* Why do you insist upon talking about other things?

ANTIGONE. I am not talking about other things.

ISMENE. Antigone, I've thought about it a lot.

ANTIGONE. Did you?

ISMENE. I thought about it all night long. Antigone, you're mad.

ANTIGONE. Am I?

ISMENE. We cannot do it.

ANTIGONE. Why not?

ISMENE. Creon will have us put to death.

ANTIGONE. Of course he will. But we are *bound* to go out and bury our brother. That's the way it is. What do you think *we* can do to change it?

ISMENE. *(Releases* ANTIGONE's *hand; draws back a step)* I don't want to die.

ANTIGONE. I'd prefer not to die, myself. (ANTIGONE *crosses below the table over to front of upstage part of arch Left; faces toward the arch.)*

ISMENE. *(Backs away a few steps Right as she turns to* ANTIGONE) Listen to me, Antigone. I thought about it all night. I may be younger than you are, but I always think things over, and you don't.

ANTIGONE. Sometimes it is better *not* to think too much.

ISMENE. I don't agree with you! (ISMENE *moves to upper Right end of table and leans on end of table top, toward* ANTIGONE) Oh, I know it's horrble. I *know* Polynices was cheated out of his rights. That he made war—that Creon took sides against him, and he was killed. And I pity Polynices just as much as you do. But all the same, I sort of see what Uncle Creon means. Uncle Creon is the *king* now. He *has* to set an example!

ANTIGONE. *(Turns to* ISMENE) Example! Creon orders that our brother rot and putrefy, and be mangled by dogs and birds of prey. That's an offense against every decent human instinct; against the laws of God and Man. And you talk about examples!

ISMENE. There you go, off on your own again—re-

fusing to pay the slightest heed to anybody. At least
you might try to understand!

ANTIGONE. I only understand that a man lies rotting,
unburied. And that he is my brother, (*She moves to
chair L. of the table*) and that he must be buried.

ISMENE. But Creon won't let us bury him. And he is
stronger than we are. He is the king. He has made himself King.

ANTIGONE. (*Sits*) I am not listening to you.

ISMENE. (*Kneels on stool, facing toward* ANTIGONE)
You *must!* You know how Creon works. His mob will
come running, howling as it runs. A thousand arms will
seize our arms. A thousand breaths will breathe into
our faces. Like one single pair of eyes, a thousand eyes
will stare at us. We'll be driven in a tumbril through
their hatred, through the smell of them and their cruel
roaring laughter. We'll be dragged to the scaffold for
torture, surrounded by guards with their idiot faces all
bloated, their animal hands clean-washed for the sac-
rifice, their beefy eyes squinting as they stare at us.
And we'll know that no shrieking and no begging will
make them understand that we want to live, for they
are like trained beasts who go through the motions
they've been taught, without caring about right or
wrong. And we shall suffer, we shall feel pain rising
in us until it becomes so unbearable that we *know* it
must stop: but it won't stop: it will go on rising and
rising, like a screaming voice— (ANTIGONE *suddenly
sits erect.* ISMENE *sinks down onto the stool, buries her
face in her hands and sobs*) Oh, I can't, I can't, Antigone!

(*A pause.*)

ANTIGONE. How well you have thought it all out.

ISMENE. I thought of it all night long. Didn't you?

ANTIGONE. Oh, yes.

ISMENE. I'm an awful coward, Antigone.

ANTIGONE. So am I. But what has that to do with it?

ISMENE. *(Raises her head; stares at* ANTIGONE*)* But Antigone! Don't you *want* to go on living?

ANTIGONE. Go on living! Who was always the first out of bed every morning because she loved the touch of the cold morning air on her bare skin? *(She rises; goes to Left of* ISMENE*)* Or the last to bed because nothing less than infinite weariness could wean her from the lingering night?

ISMENE. *(Clasps* ANTIGONE'S *hands, in a sudden rush of tenderness)* Antigone! My darling sister!

ANTIGONE. *(Repulsing her)* No! For pity's sakes! Don't! *(A pause as she crosses behind* ISMENE *to upstage Right Center, just below bottom step)* You say you've thought it all out. The howling mob: the torture: the fear of death: *(She turns to* ISMENE*)* they've made up your mind for you. Is that it?

ISMENE. Yes.

ANTIGONE. *All right.* They're as good excuses as any. *(*ANTIGONE *moves down to Right of* ISMENE *and stands facing Right.)*

ISMENE. *(Turns to* ANTIGONE*)* Antigone, be reasonable. It's all very well for *men* to believe in ideas, and die for them. But you are a *girl!* Antigone, you have everything in the world to make you happy. All you have to do is—reach out for it. *(She clasps* ANTIGONE'S *left hand in hers)* You are going to be married; you are young; you are beautiful—

ANTIGONE. *(Turns to* ISMENE*)* I am *not* beautiful.

ISMENE. Oh, yes, you are! Not the way other girls are. But it's always you that the little tough boys turn to look back at when they pass us in the street. And when you go by, the little girls stop talking: they stare and stare at you, until we've turned a corner.

ANTIGONE. *(A faint smile in the corner of her mouth)* "Little tough boys—little girls."

ISMENE. And what about *Haemon?*

(A pause.)

ANTIGONE. *(Looks off toward Right)* I shall see

Haemon this morning. I'll take care of Haemon. Go
back to bed now, Ismene. The sun is coming up! *(She
releases* ISMENE's *hand; crosses behind* ISMENE *to upstage Left Center)* and as you can see, there is nothing
I can do today. Our brother Polynices is as well guarded
as if he had won the war and were sitting on his throne.

ISMENE. *(Turns to her)* What are you going to do?

(The LIGHTING slowly dims up to a higher mark.)

NURSE. *(Calls from offstage Left through arch)*
Come, my dove. Come to your breakfast.

*(*ANTIGONE *and* ISMENE *glance off in the direction
whence came the* NURSE's *voice.)*

ANTIGONE. Please go back to bed.

ISMENE. *(Rises, goes to Right of* ANTIGONE, *and
grasps her by the arms)* If I do—promise me you won't
leave the house?

ANTIGONE. *(Takes* ISMENE's *hands in hers)* Very
well, then—I promise.

*(*ANTIGONE *releases* ISMENE's *hands, then* ISMENE
goes to arch Left and exits. ANTIGONE *moves down
to chair at Left end of the table.)*

NURSE. *(Enters through Left arch, speaking as she
enters, and goes to just front of the arch)* Come along.
Breakfast, my dear. *(She turns toward arch as if to
exit.)*

ANTIGONE. I'm not very hungry, nurse. *(She sits
in chair* L. *of table.)*

NURSE. *(Stops, looks at* ANTIGONE, *then moves to
behind and Left of her)* My darling— Where is your
pain?

ANTIGONE. Nowhere. But you must keep me warm
and safe, as you used to do when I was little. *(She
holds out her hand toward the* NURSE) Oh, Nanny,
give me your hand— (NURSE *gives* ANTIGONE *her*

hand) as if I were sick in bed and you were sitting beside me.

NURSE. *(Stands behind* ANTIGONE, *her right arm
around* ANTIGONE's *shoulder)* My lamb! What is it
that's eating your heart out?

ANTIGONE. Nothing. It's just that I'm not quite
strong enough for what I have to do. But nobody but
you must know that.

NURSE. *(Places her other arm around* ANTIGONE's
shoulder) Not strong enough for what, my kitten?

(A light blue color begins to lighten up the cyclorama.)

ANTIGONE. Nothing. Oh, it's so good that you are
here. I can hold your calloused hand that is so prompt
and strong to ward off evil. You are very powerful,
Nanny.

NURSE. What is it you want me to do for you, my
baby?

ANTIGONE. There isn't anything to do—except: put
your hand like this—against my cheek. *(She places
the* NURSE's *hand against her cheek. A pause, then, as*
ANTIGONE *leans back, her eyes shut.* NURSE *strokes*
ANTIGONE's *hair with her other hand)* I'm not afraid
any more.

NURSE. There!

ANTIGONE. *(A pause. Then* ANTIGONE *resumes on
another note)* Nanny—

NURSE. *(Leans forward)* Yes?

ANTIGONE. My dog, Puff—

NURSE. *(Straightens up; draws her hand away)*
Well?

ANTIGONE. Promise me that you won't ever scold
her again.

NURSE. Dogs that dirty up a house with their filthy
paws *(She crosses behind* ANTIGONE *to Right of her)*
deserve to be scolded.

ANTIGONE. And promise me that you will talk to her.
That you will talk to her often,

NURSE. *(Turns and looks at* ANTIGONE*) Me,* talk to a dog!

ANTIGONE. But you are not to talk to her the way people usually talk to dogs. You're to talk to her the way I talk to her.

NURSE. I don't see why the both of us should make fools of ourselves. So long as *you're* here, *one* ought to be enough.

ANTIGONE. But if there was some reason *why* I couldn't go on talking to her—

NURSE. *(Interrupting)* Couldn't go on talking to her! And why couldn't you go on talking to her? Now what kind of poppycock is this, I'd like to know—

ANTIGONE. *(Breaks in, averting her head and taking hold of herself)* And if she got too unhappy; if she moaned and moaned, waiting for me with her nose under the door the way she does when I'm out all day; then the best thing, Nanny, might be to have her mercifully put to sleep.

NURSE. Now what *has* got into you this morning? (HAEMON *enters through arch Right and crosses to Right Center)* Running round in the darkness, won't sleep, won't eat— (ANTIGONE *sees* HAEMON*)* and now it's your *dog* she wants killed. I never—

ANTIGONE. *(Interrupting; rises and grasps* NURSE *by the arms)* Nanny! Haemon is here. Go inside, please. And don't forget what you've promised.

*(*NURSE *goes to arch Left and exits.* ANTIGONE *goes to above and Right of the table. A pause.)*

ANTIGONE. Haemon, Haemon! Forgive me for quarreling with you last night. *(She crosses quickly to Left of* HAEMON*)* Forgive me for everything. It was all my fault. (HAEMON *moves a few steps toward her. They embrace)* Oh, I beg you to forgive me.

HAEMON. You know that I've forgiven you. You had hardly slammed the door; your perfume still hung in the room, when I had already forgiven you. *(He holds her in his arms and smiles at her)* You stole that perfume. From whom?

ANTIGONE. Ismene.

HAEMON. And the rouge, and the face powder, and the dress?

ANTIGONE. Ismene.

HAEMON. And in whose honor did you get yourself up so glamorously?

ANTIGONE. I'll tell you. *(She draws him closer)* Oh, what a fool I was! To waste a whole evening! A whole, beautiful evening!

HAEMON. We'll have other evenings, my sweet.

ANTIGONE. Perhaps we won't.

HAEMON. And other quarrels, too. A happy love is full of quarrels.

ANTIGONE. A happy love, yes. Haemon, listen to me.

HAEMON. Yes?

ANTIGONE. And don't laugh at me this morning. Be serious.

HAEMON. I am serious.

ANTIGONE. And hold me tight. *Tighter* than you have ever held me. I want all your strength to flow into me.

(They embrace closer. His cheek against her upstage cheek.)

HAEMON. *There!* With all my strength.

(A pause.)

ANTIGONE. *(Breathless)* That's good. *(They stand for a moment, silent and motionless)* Haemon! I wanted to tell you. You know— The little boy we were going to have when we were married?

HAEMON. Yes?

ANTIGONE. I'd have protected him against everything in the world.

HAEMON. Yes, dear sweet.

ANTIGONE. Oh, you don't know how I should have held him in my arms and given him my strength. He wouldn't have been afraid of anything, Haemon. His mother wouldn't have been very imposing: her hair wouldn't have been very well brushed; but she would have been strong where he was concerned, so much stronger than any other mother in the world. You believe that, don't you, Haemon?

HAEMON. Yes, my dearest.

ANTIGONE. And you believe me when I say that *you* would have had a real wife?

HAEMON. *(Draws her into his arms)* I *have* a real wife.

ANTIGONE. *(Pressing against him and crying out)* Haemon, you loved me! You *did* love me that night. You're sure of it!

HAEMON. What night, my sweet?

ANTIGONE. And you are sure that that night, at the dance, when you came to the corner where I was sitting, there was no mistake? It was *me* you were looking for? It wasn't another girl? And that not in your secret heart of hearts, have you said to yourself that it was Ismene you ought to have asked to marry you?

HAEMON. *(Reproachfully)* Antigone, you are idiotic. *(He kisses her.)*

ANTIGONE. Oh, you do love me, don't you? You love me as a woman—as a woman wants to be loved, don't you? Your arms around me aren't lying, are they? Your hands, so warm against my back—they aren't lies? This warmth; this strength that flows through me as I stand so close to you. They aren't lies, are they?

HAEMON. Antigone, my darling—I love you. *(He kisses her again.)*

ANTIGONE. *(Turns her head partly away from him)* I'm sallow—and I'm not pretty. Ismene is pink and golden. She's like a fruit.

HAEMON. Antigone—!

ANTIGONE. Oh, forgive me, I am ashamed of myself. But this morning, this special morning, I must know. Tell me the truth! I beg you to tell me the truth! When you think of me, when it strikes you suddenly that I am going to belong to you— *(She looks at him)* do you get the sense that—that a great *empty* space—is being hollowed out inside you; and that there is something inside you that is just—dying?

HAEMON. Yes, I do.

(A pause as they face against one another.)

ANTIGONE. That's the way I feel. *(She clings to him for a moment)* There! And now I have two things more to tell you. And when I have told them to you, you must go away instantly, without asking any questions. However strange they may seem to you. However much they may hurt you. Swear that you will!

(A pause, as HAEMON kisses her hand.)

HAEMON. *(Beginning to be troubled)* What are these things that you are going to tell me?

ANTIGONE. Swear, first, that you will go away without a single word. Without so much as looking at me. *(She looks at him, wretchedness in her face)* You hear me, Haemon. Swear, please. It's the last *mad* wish that you will ever have to grant me.

(A pause.)

HAEMON. I swear it.

ANTIGONE. Thank you. Well, here it is. First, about last night, when I went to your house. You asked me a moment ago *why* I wore Ismene's dress and rouge. I did it because I was stupid. I wasn't sure that you loved me—as a woman; and I did it because I wanted you to want me.

HAEMON. Was *that* the reason? Oh, my poor—

ANTIGONE. *(Places her hand on his face)* No! Wait! That was the reason. And you laughed at me, and we quarreled, and I flung out of the house. The reason why I went to your house last night was that I wanted you to take me. I wanted to be your wife—before.

HAEMON. *(Questioningly)* Antigone—?

ANTIGONE. *(Shuts him off; places both hands on his face)* Haemon! You swore you wouldn't ask a single question. You swore it, Haemon. As a matter of fact, I'll tell you why. I wanted to be your wife last night because I love you that way very—very strongly. And also—because— Oh, my beloved— *(She removes her hands from his face)* I'm going to cause you such a lot of pain. I wanted it also because *(She draws a step away from him)* I shall never—never be able to marry you, never!

HAEMON. *(Moves a step toward her)* Antigone—!

ANTIGONE. *(She moves a few steps away from him)* Haemon! You took a solemn oath! You swore! Leave me now! Tomorrow the whole thing will be clear to you. Even before tomorrow: this afternoon. *(He makes a slight gesture toward her)* If you *please*, Haemon, go now. It's the only thing left that you can do for me if you still love me. *(A pause as HAEMON stares at her. Then he turns and goes out through the arch Right. ANTIGONE stands motionless. In a strange, gentle voice, as of calm after the storm, she speaks:)* Well, it's over for Haemon, Antigone.

ISMENE. *(Enters through arch Left, pauses for a moment in front of it when she sees ANTIGONE, then crosses behind table to Right end of it)* I can't sleep. I'm terrified. *(ANTIGONE sits chair Right of table)* I'm so afraid that even though it is daylight, you'll still try to bury Polynices. *(ISMENE kneels down on the floor, at the Left side of chair where ANTIGONE is seated. ANTIGONE looks at ISMENE)* Antigone, you know I love you: you know I want you to be happy. And you remember what he was like. He was our brother, *(ANTIGONE looks off Right through the arch)* of course. But he's dead; and he never loved us. He was a bad brother. He was like an enemy in this house. He never thought of you: why should you think of him? What if he does have to lie rotting in a field? *(ANTIGONE rises; moves toward the arch Right)* It's Creon's doing, not ours. *(ISMENE stands up; moves around behind chair Right over to Left of ANTIGONE)* Don't try to change things. You can't bury Polynices. I won't let you!

ANTIGONE. *(Stops in front of arch, turns and looks at* ISMENE*)* You are too late, Ismene. When you first saw me this morning, I had just come in from burying him. (ANTIGONE *exits through arch Right.)*

(ISMENE *reacts, then runs out arch Right after* AN-TIGONE. *The LIGHTING is quickly dimmed out, leaving the stage bathed in a light blue color. In the distance, a CLOCK is heard striking One. The LIGHTS are quickly brought up to suggest a later period of the day.* CREON *and the* PAGE *enter through curtain upstage Center.* CREON *stands on the top step, his* PAGE *stands on his Right side, one step below* CREON.*)*

CREON. A private of the guards, you say? (CREON *moves down to behind the table)* One of those standing watch over the body? Show him in.

(The PAGE *crosses to arch Right and exits. A pause, then the first* GUARD, *livid with fear, enters through Right arch, followed by the* PAGE. *The* GUARD *is hatless.* PAGE *remains on upstage side of arch Right.* GUARD *goes to behind chair Right of table, and salutes.)*

GUARD. Private Jonas, Second Battalion.

CREON. What are you doing here? (CREON *turns away from* GUARD.*)*

GUARD. It's like this, Chief. Soon as it happened, we said: "Got to tell the Chief about this before anybody else spills it. He'll want to know right away." So we tossed a coin to see which one would come up and tell you about it. You see, Chief, we thought only one man better come, because after all you don't want to leave the body without a guard. Right? I mean, there's three of us on duty. Guarding the body.

CREON. The body? What's wrong about the body?

GUARD. Chief, I've been seventeen years in the service. Volunteer: two citations. My record's clean. I know my business and I know my place. I carry out orders. Sir, ask any officer in the battalion, they'll tell you. "Leave it to Jonas. Give him an order: he'll carry it out." That's what they'll tell you, Chief. Jonas, that's me—that's my name.

CREON. *(Moves down Left end of table to below it)* What's the matter with you, man? What are you shaking for?

GUARD. By rights it's the corporal's job, Chief. I've been recommended for a corporal but they haven't put it through yet. June, it was supposed to go through. *(He becomes rattled)* But with all this red tape and—

CREON. *(Interrupts)* Stop chattering and tell me why you are here. If anything has gone wrong with that body I'll break all three of you.

GUARD. Nobody can say we didn't keep our eye on that body. We had the two o'clock watch: the tough one. You know how it is, Chief. It's nearly the end of the night. Your eyes are like lead. You've got a crick in the back of your neck. There's shadows, and the fog is beginning to roll in. A fine watch they give us! And me, seventeen years in the service. But, we was doing our duty, all right. On our feet, all of us. Anybody says we were sleeping is a liar. First place, it was too cold. Second place—

CREON. *(Makes a gesture of impatience, turns and goes upstage to the top step, Center)* Ahh!

GUARD. Yes, Chief. Well, I turned round and looked at the body. We wasn't only ten feet away from it, but that's how I am. I was keeping my eye on it. (CREON *turns toward the* GUARD, *who shouts)* Listen, Chief, I was the first man to see it! Me! They'll tell you. I was the one let out that yell!

CREON. What for? What was the matter?

GUARD. Chief, the *body!* Somebody had been there and buried him.

CREON. *(Moves down a step toward the* GUARD*)* My God, I'll—!

GUARD. *(The* GUARD *becomes more frightened)* It wasn't much, you understand. With us three there, it couldn't have been. Just covered over with a little dirt, that's all. But enough to hide it from the buzzards.

CREON. *(Looks intently at the* GUARD*)* You are sure that it couldn't have been—a dog, scratching up the earth?

GUARD. Not a chance, Chief. That's kind of what we hoped it was. But the earth was scattered over the body just like the priests tell you you should do it. Whoever did that job knew what he was doing, all right.

CREON. Who could have dared?— *(He turns and moves down to behind Left end of the table)* Was there any indication as to who might have done it?

GUARD. *(Moves downstage to Right of* CREON*)* Not a thing, Chief. Maybe we heard a footstep. I can't swear to it. Of course we started right in to search, and the corporal found a shovel, a kid's shovel no bigger than that, all rusty and everything. Corporal's got the shovel for you. We thought maybe a kid did it.

CREON. *(To* GUARD*)* A kid!— *(He looks away from the* GUARD. *To himself)* I broke the back of the rebellion; but like a snake, it is coming together again. *(He moves away to upper Left end of the table)* Polynices' friends, with their gold, blocked by my orders, in the banks of Thebes. The leaders of the populace, allied to envious princes. And the temple priests, always ready for a bit of fishing in troubled waters. A *kid! (He sits on the stool)* I can imagine what he is like, their kid: a baby-faced killer, creeping in the night with a toy shovel under his jacket. *(He looks at his* PAGE*)* Though why shouldn't they have corrupted a *real* child? *There* is something, now, to soften the hearts and weaken the minds of the people! Very touching! Very useful to them, an innocent child. A martyr. A real white-faced baby of fourteen who will spit with contempt at the guards who kill him. A free gift to their cause: the precious, innocent blood of a child on my hands. *(He holds his hands out and looks at them)* They must have accomplices in the Guard itself. *(He looks at the* GUARD, *who reacts)* Look here, you. Who knows about this?

GUARD. Only us three, Chief. We flipped a coin, and I came right over.

CREON. Right. Listen, now. You will continue on duty. When the relief squad comes up, you will tell them to return to barracks. You will uncover the body; keep a sharp watch, and if another attempt is made to give the corpse burial, you will make an arrest and bring the prisoner straight to me. And you will keep your mouths shut about this. Not one word to a human soul. *(He rises)* You are all guilty of neglect of duty, and you will be punished; but if the rumor spreads through Thebes that the body received burial, you will be shot—all three of you.

GUARD. *(Excitedly)* Chief, we never told nobody, I swear we didn't. Anyhow, I've been up here. Suppose my pals spilled it to the relief; I couldn't have been with them and here, too. That wouldn't be my fault, if they talked. Chief, I've got two kids. You're my witness, Chief, it couldn't have been me. I was here with you. *(He begins to shout, excitedly)* I've got a witness. If anybody talked, it couldn't have been me! I was—

CREON. *(Interrupts) Clear out!* If the story doesn't get round, you won't be shot. (GUARD *salutes, turns and exits through Right arch on the run.* CREON *goes up to the top step Center, stands there, musing)* A *child!* (CREON *looks at his* PAGE) Come here, my boy. *(The* PAGE *crosses to Right side of* CREON; *stands on the second step)* Would you defy me with your little shovel? (PAGE *looks up at him.* CREON *turns away)* Of course you would. You would do it, too. (CREON *murmurs) A child!*

(CREON *looks toward the vent in curtain; the* PAGE *draws aside the curtain through which* CREON *exits,* PAGE *behind him.)*

(A pause.)

(The CHORUS *enters through Left arch, glances toward*

place CREON *has exited, then he moves to down-stage Left Center, below chair Left of table. The* CHORUS *allows a pause to indicate that a crucial moment has been reached in the play.)*

CHORUS. And now the spring is wound up *tight! (He gestures with a clenched fist)* It will uncoil of itself. *(He moves to below the table)* That is what is so convenient in tragedy. The least little turn of the wrist will do the job. Anything will set it going: a glance at a girl who happens to be lifting her arm to her hair as you go by; a feeling when you wake up on a fine morning that you'd like a little respect paid to you today, as if it were as easy to order as a second cup of coffee; one question too many, idly thrown out over a friendly drink—and the tragedy is on. The rest is automatic. You don't need to lift a finger. The machine is in perfect order: it has been oiled ever since time began, and it runs without friction. Death, treason, and sorrow, are on the march; and they move in the wake of storm, of tears, of stillness. *(He moves Right a few steps)* Every kind of stillness. The *hush*—when the executioner's axe goes up at the end of the last act. The—*unbreathable* —silence when, at the beginning of the play, the two lovers, their hearts bared, their bodies naked, stand for the first time—face to face in the darkened room, afraid to stir. The silence *inside* you when the roaring crowd acclaims the winner—so that you think of a film without a sound-track, mouths agape and no sound coming out of them, a clamor that is no more than a picture; and *you,* the victor, *(He points toward the audience)* already vanquished, alone in the desert of your silence. That is tragedy. (CHORUS *moves over to below the chair at Right end of the table)* Tragedy is clean, it is firm, it is flawless. It has nothing to do with melodrama —with wicked villains, persecuted maidens, avengers, gleams of hope and eleventh-hour repentances. Death, in a melodrama, is really horrible because it is never inevitable. The dear old father might so easily have been saved; the honest young man might so easily have brought in the police five minutes earlier. *(The LIGHT-ING dims up to the highest level of the play; suggesting mid-afternoon.* CHORUS *moves over to downstage Right Center)* In a tragedy, nothing is in doubt and everyone's destiny is known. That makes for tranquility. Tragedy is restful; and the reason is that *hope,* that foul, deceitful thing, has no part in it. There isn't any hope. You're trapped. The whole sky has fallen on you, and all you can do about it is to shout. (CHORUS *starts moving across to downstage Left Center)* Now don't mistake me: I said "shout": I did not say groan, whimper, complain. *That,* you cannot do. But you can *shout* aloud; you can get all those things said that you never thought you'd be able to say—or never even knew you had it in you to say. And you don't say these things because it will do any good to say them: you know better than that. You say them for their own sake; you say them because you learn a lot from them. (CHORUS *goes over to front of arch Left)* In melodrama, you argue and struggle in the hope of escape. That is vulgar; it's practical. But in tragedy, where there is no temptation to try to escape, argument is gratuitous: it's kingly. *(Voices of the* GUARDS *and scuffling sounds heard from off Right through the archway.* CHORUS *looks in that direction, then in a changed tone, speaks)* The play is on. Antigone has been caught. For the first time in her life, Antigone is going to be able to be herself. (CHORUS *exits through arch Left.)*

(A pause, while the offstage voices rise in volume, then the FIRST GUARD *enters through arch Right, followed by* SECOND *and* THIRD GUARDS, *holding the arms of* ANTIGONE *and dragging her along.* SECOND GUARD *is on the downstage side of* ANTIGONE, *the* THIRD GUARD *on her upstage side, grasping her handcuffed hand. The* FIRST GUARD, *speaking as he enters, crosses swiftly to above the Right end of the table. The* TWO GUARDS *and* ANTIGONE *stop downstage Right Center.)*

FIRST GUARD. *(Recovered from his fright)* Come on, now, Miss, give it a rest. The Chief will be here in a minute and you can tell him about it. All I know is my orders. *(He turns to* ANTIGONE*)* I don't want to know what you were doing there. People always have excuses; but I can't afford to listen to them, see. Say, if we had to listen to all the people who want to tell us what's the matter with this country, we'd never get our work done.

ANTIGONE. They are hurting me. Tell them to take their dirty hands off me.

FIRST GUARD. *(Moves down to below Left end of table)* Dirty hands, eh? And what about stiffs, and dirt, and such like. You wasn't afraid to touch them, was you? "Their dirty hands!" Take a look at your *own* hands!

ANTIGONE. Tell them to let me go. I shan't run away. My father was King Oedipus. I am Antigone.

FIRST GUARD. *(Moves to below Right end of table)* King Oedipus' little girl! What do you know about that! Listen, Miss, the night watch never picks up a lady, but they say, you better be careful; I'm sleeping with the police commissioner. *(The other* GUARDS *laugh.* ANTIGONE, *handcuffed, smiles despite herself as she looks down at her hands. They are grubby)* Guess you must have lost your shovel, didn't you? *(He crosses to below chair at Right end of the table)* Had to go at it with your finger-nails the second time, I guess. By God, I never saw such nerve! I turned my back for about five seconds and there she is, clawing away like a hyena. And boy! Did she scratch and kick when I grabbed her? Straight for my eyes with them nails, she went. And yelling something fierce about, "I ain't finished yet; let me finish!" *(To the other* GUARDS*)* You keep hold of her and I'll see that she keeps her face shut!

SECOND GUARD. Don't worry. She won't get away this time!

FIRST GUARD. Listen, we're going to get a bonus out

of this. What do you say we throw a party, the three of us?

SECOND GUARD. At the old woman's? Behind Market Street?

THIRD GUARD. Suits me. Sunday would be a good day. We're off duty Sunday. And what do you say: we bring the *wives?*

FIRST GUARD. Nix. Let's have some fun this time. Bring your wife, and they always put the damper on! *(He moves a few steps toward them)* Say, listen. Who would have thought an hour ago that us three would be talking about throwing a party right now? The way I felt when the old man was interrogatin' me, we'd be lucky if we got off with being docked a month's pay. I want to tell you, I was scared.

SECOND GUARD. You sure we're going to get a bonus?

FIRST GUARD. *(Turns, goes below table to below chair at Left end of the table)* Yeah. Something tells me *this* is big stuff.

THIRD GUARD. *(To SECOND GUARD)* What's-his-name, you know—in the Third Battalion? He got an extra month's pay for catching a fire-bug.

SECOND GUARD. If we get an extra month's pay, I vote we throw the party at the Arabian's.

FIRST GUARD. You're crazy! He charges twice as much for liquor as anybody else in town. Unless you want to go upstairs, of course. Can't do that at the old woman's.

THIRD GUARD. Say, we ain't going to do so hot, no matter how you figure it. You get an extra month's pay, and what happens? Everybody in the outfit knows it, and your wife knows it too. They might even line up the battalion and give it to you in front of everybody.

FIRST GUARD. Well, we'll see about that. If they do the job out in the barracks-yard—of course that means women, kids, everything.

ANTIGONE. *(Meekly)* I should like to sit down, if you please.

(A pause, as the FIRST GUARD thinks it over.)

FIRST GUARD. Let her sit down. But keep hold of her. *(The TWO GUARDS start leading her toward the chair at Right end of table. The vent upstage Center opens, and CREON enters, followed by his PAGE. FIRST GUARD turns and moves upstage a few steps, sees CREON)* 'Tenshun!

(The THREE GUARDS salute. CREON, seeing ANTIGONE handcuffed to THIRD GUARD, stops on the top step, astonished.)

CREON. *(To ANTIGONE)* Antigone! What is this? *(To the FIRST GUARD)* Take off those handcuffs! *(FIRST GUARD crosses above table to Left of AN-TIGONE)* What is this?

(FIRST GUARD takes key from his pocket and unlocks the cuff on ANTIGONE'S hand. ANTIGONE rubs her wrist, crosses below table toward chair at Left end of table. SECOND and THIRD GUARDS step back to front of arch Right. FIRST GUARD, above chair Right of table, turns upstage toward CREON.)

FIRST GUARD. The watch, Chief. We all came this time.
CREON. Who is guarding the body?
FIRST GUARD. We sent for the relief.
CREON. *(Moves down to Left of FIRST GUARD)* But I gave orders that the relief was to go back to barracks and stay there! *(ANTIGONE sits on chair Left of table. PAGE remains on the second step, upstage Center)* I told you not to open your mouth about this!
GUARD. Nobody's said anything, Chief. But acting on your orders, we made this arrest, and brought the party in.
CREON. *(Moves to upper Left end of table. To AN-TIGONE)* Where did these men find *you?*
FIRST GUARD. Right by the body.
CREON. What were you doing near your brother's body? You knew what my orders were.

FIRST GUARD. What was she doing? Chief, that's why we brought her in. She was digging up the dirt with her nails. She was trying to cover up the body all over again.

CREON. *(Turns a step toward the* GUARD*)* Do you realize what you are saying?

FIRST GUARD. Chief, ask these men here. After I reported to you, I went back, and first thing we did, we uncovered the body. The sun was coming up and it was beginning to smell. So we moved him up on a little rise to get him in the wind. Of course you wouldn't expect any trouble in broad daylight. But just the same, we decided one of us better keep his eye peeled all the time. About noon, what with the sun and the smell, being the wind dropped, and I wasn't feeling none too good, I went over to my pal to get a chew. I just had time to say "thanks" and stick it in my mouth, when I turn round and there she is clawing away at the dirt with both hands. Right out in broad daylight! Wouldn't you think when she saw me come running she'd quit and beat it out of there? Not *her!* She went right on digging as fast as she could, as if I weren't there at all. And when I grabbed her, she scratched and bit and yelled to leave her alone, she hadn't finished yet, the body wasn't all covered yet, and the like of that!

CREON. *(To* ANTIGONE*)* Is this true?

ANTIGONE. Yes, it is true.

FIRST GUARD. We scraped the dirt off as fast as we could, then we sent for the relief and we posted them. But we didn't tell them a thing, Chief. And we brought her to the party so's you could see her. And that's the truth so help me God.

CREON. (*To* ANTIGONE.) And was it *you* who covered the body the first time? In the night?

ANTIGONE. Yes, it was. With a toy shovel we used to take to the seashore when we were children. It was Polynices' own shovel: he had cut his name in the handle. That was why I left it with him. But these men took it away; so the next time, I had to do it with my hands.

FIRST GUARD. *(Above chair Right of table)* Chief, she was clawing away like a wild animal. Matter of fact, first minute we saw her, what with the heat haze and everything, my pal says, "That must be a dog," he says. "Dog!" I says; that's a *girl*, that is!" And it was.

CREON. *(Looks over his shoulder at* FIRST GUARD*)* Very well. *(Turns and goes upstage Center to below step, speaks to the* PAGE*)* Show these men to the ante-room. *(The* PAGE *crosses to the upstage side of arch Right, stands there, waiting.* CREON *moves to behind the table. To the* FIRST GUARD*)* You three men will wait outside. I may want a report from you later.

FIRST GUARD. Do I put the cuffs back on her, Chief?

CREON. No. *(The* THREE GUARDS *salute, do an about-face and exit through arch Right.* SECOND *and* THIRD GUARDS *go out first, followed by the* FIRST GUARD. *The* PAGE *follows him out. A long pause.* CREON *moves to Right Center, looks off through arch)* Had you told anybody what you meant to do?

ANTIGONE. No.

CREON. Did you meet anyone on your way—coming or going?

ANTIGONE. No, nobody.

CREON. You're quite sure of that?

ANTIGONE. Quite sure.

CREON. *(Turns and moves to upper Right end of table)* Very well. Now listen to me. You will go straight to your room. When you get there, you will go to bed. You will say that you are not well and that you have not been out since yesterday. Your nurse will tell the same story. *(He looks toward arch Right, through which the* GUARDS *have exited)* And I'll dispose of those three men.

ANTIGONE. Uncle Creon, there's no reason to kill those three guards. You *must* know that I'll do it all over again tonight.

(A pause. They look one another in the eye.)

CREON. Why did you try to bury your brother?

ANTIGONE. I owed it to him.

CREON. I had forbidden it.

ANTIGONE. I owed it to him. Those who are not buried wander eternally and find no rest. Everybody knows that. I owed it to him to unlock the house of the dead in which my father and my mother are waiting to welcome him. Polynices has earned his rest.

CREON. Polynices was a rebel and a traitor, and you know it.

ANTIGONE. He was my brother.

CREON. You heard my edict. It was proclaimed throughout Thebes. You *read* my edict. It was posted up on the city walls.

ANTIGONE. Yes.

CREON. You know the punishment I decreed for any person who attempted to give him burial.

ANTIGONE. Yes, I know the punishment.

CREON. Did you by any chance *act* on the assumption that a daughter of Oedipus, a daughter of Oedipus' stubborn pride, was *above* the law?

ANTIGONE. I did not act on that assumption.

CREON. Because if you had acted on that assumption, Antigone, you would have been deeply wrong. Nobody has a more sacred obligation to *obey* the law than those who *make* the law. You are a daughter of law-makers, a daughter of kings. You must observe the law.

ANTIGONE. Had I been a scullery maid washing my dishes when that law was read aloud to me, I should have scrubbed the greasy water from my arms and gone out in my apron to bury my brother.

CREON. What nonsense! If you had been a scullery maid, there would have been no doubt in your mind about the seriousness of that edict. You would have known that it meant death; and you would have been satisfied to weep for your brother in your kitchen. *(He paces upstage a few steps)* But *you!* You thought that because you come of the royal line, *(He returns to chair Right of the table)* because you were my niece and were going to marry my son, I shouldn't dare have you killed.

ANTIGONE. You are mistaken. I never doubted for an instant that you would have me put to death.

(A pause, as CREON stares fixedly at her.)

CREON. The pride of Oedipus! Oedipus and his headstrong pride all over again. I can see your father in you—and I believe you. *(He moves to upper Right end of the table)* Of course you thought that I should have you killed! Proud as you are, it seemed to you a natural climax in your existence. Your father was like that. For *him*, as for *you*, human happiness was meaningless; and mere human misery was not enough to satisfy his passion for torment. You come of people for whom the human vestment is a kind of strait-jacket: it cracks at the seams: You spend your lives wriggling to get out of it. Nothing less than a cosy tea-party with death and destiny will quench your thirst. *(He sits on stool behind the table)* The happiest hour of your father's life came when he listened *greedily* to the story of how, unknown to himself, he had killed his own father and dishonored the bed of his own mother. Drop by drop, word by word, he drank in the dark story that the gods had destined him, first to live and then to *hear*. How avidly men and women drink the brew of such a tale when their names are Oedipus— and Antigone! And it is so simple, afterwards, to do what your father did, to put out his eyes and take you, his daughter, begging on the highways. Let me tell you this, Antigone: those days are over for Thebes. Thebes has a right to a king without a past. My name, thank God, is only Creon. I stand here with both feet firm on the ground; with both hands in my pockets; and I have decided that so long as *I* am king—being less ambitious than your father was—I shall merely devote myself to introducing a little order into this absurd kingdom —if that is possible. Don't think that being a king seems to me romantic. It is my trade; a trade a man has to work at every day; and like every other trade, it isn't all beer and skittles. But since it is my trade, I mean to take it seriously. And if, tomorrow, some wild and bearded messenger walks in from some wild and distant valley—which is what happened to your father—and tells me that he's not quite sure who my parents were, but thinks that my wife Eurydice is actually my mother, I shall ask him to do me the kindness to go back where he came from; and I shan't let a little matter like *that* persuade me to order my wife to take a blood test or the police to let me know whether or not my birth certificate was forged. *Kings*, my girl, have other things to do than to surrender themselves to their private feelings. *(He looks at her and smiles)* Hand *you* over to be killed! *(He rises, moves to Left end of table)* I have *other* plans for you. You're going to marry Haemon, and you're going to give him a sturdy boy. *(He sits on the table top)* Let me assure you that Thebes needs that boy a good deal more than it needs your death. Now, you will go straight to your room and do as you have been told; and not a word about this to anybody. Don't fret about the guards; I'll see that their mouths are shut. And don't annihilate me with those eyes. I know that you think I am a brute, and I'm sure you must consider me very prosaic. But the fact is, I have always been fond of you, stubborn though you always were. Don't forget that the first doll you ever had came from me. *(A pause. ANTIGONE says nothing, rises and crosses slowly below the table toward the arch Right. CREON truns and watches her; then:)* Where are you going?

ANTIGONE. *(Stops downstage Right Center, front of the arch. Without any show of rebellion)* You know very well where I am going.

CREON. *(After a pause)* What sort of game are you playing?

ANTIGONE. I am not playing games.

CREON. *(Stands up, remains at Left end of table)* Antigone, don't you realize that if apart from those three guards—a single soul finds out what you have tried to do, it will be impossible for me to avoid putting you to death? There is still a chance that I can save you; but *only* if you keep this to yourself and give up your crazy purpose. Five minutes more, and it will be too late.

ANTIGONE. I must go out and bury my brother. Those men have uncovered him.

CREON. What good will it do? You know that there are *other* men standing guard over Polynice's body. And even if you did cover him over with earth again, the earth would again be removed.

ANTIGONE. *(Moves a step Left)* I know all that. But that much, at least I can do. And what a person can do, a person should do.

CREON. Tell me, Antigone, *(Moves below table to lower Right end)* do you believe all that flummery about religious burial? Do you really believe that a so-called shade of your brother is condemned to wander forever homeless if a *little* earth is not flung on his corpse to the accompaniment of some priestly abracadabra? *(He sits in chair at Right end of table)* Have you ever listened to the priests of Thebes when they were mumbling their formula? Have you ever watched their dreary sullen faces while they were preparing the dead for burial—skipping half the gestures required by the ritual, swallowing half their words, hustling the dead into their graves out of fear that they might be late for lunch?

ANTIGONE. Yes, I have seen all that.

CREON. And did you never say to yourself as you watched them, that if someone you really loved lay dead under the shuffling, mumbling ministrations of the priests— *(He stands up, moves to lower Right end of the table)* you would scream aloud and beg the priests to leave the dead in peace?

ANTIGONE. No, Creon. There is God and there are His priests. (CREON *turns to her*) And they are not the same thing. You are not free to do with men as you wish—not even when they are dead.

CREON. And you are going to *stop* me, are you?

ANTIGONE. Yes, I am going to stop you.

(A pause as they stand looking at one another.)

CREON. You must want very much to die. You look like a trapped animal.

ANTIGONE. Stop feeling sorry for me. Do as I do. Do your job. But if you are a human being, do it quickly.

CREON. I want to *save* you, Antigone.

ANTIGONE. You are the king, and you are all powerful. But *that* you cannot do.

CREON. You think not?

ANTIGONE. Neither *save* me nor *stop* me.

CREON. Prideful Antigone!

ANTIGONE. Only this can you do: have me put to death.

CREON. Have you *tortured*, perhaps?

ANTIGONE. Why should you do that? To see me cry? To hear me beg for mercy? Or swear whatever you wish, and then begin over again?

(A pause. Then CREON *crosses to Left of* ANTIGONE.*)*

CREON. You listen to me. You have cast me for the villain in this little play of yours, and yourself for the heroine. And you know it, you damned little mischief-maker! *(He turns and moves to upstage Right Center)* But don't you drive me too far! *(He turns to her)* If I were one of your preposterous little tyrants that Greece is full of, you would be lying in a ditch this minute with your tongue pulled out and your body drawn and quartered. *(He moves down to Left of her)* But you can see *something* in my face that makes me hesitate to send for the guards and turn you over to them. Instead, I let you go on arguing; and you taunt me, you take the offensive. *(He grasps her left hand by the wrist)* What are you driving at, you she-devil? *(He twists her arm,)*

ANTIGONE. Let me go. You are hurting my arm.

CREON. *(Gripping her tighter)* I will not let you go.
ANTIGONE. *(Moans)* Oh!—
CREON. I should have done this from the beginning.
I was a fool to waste words. *(He looks at her)* I may
be your uncle; but we are not a particularly affection-
ate family. Are we, eh? *(Through his teeth as he
twists) Are we?* (CREON *twists her left arm so forcibly
that* ANTIGONE, *wincing with pain, is propelled round
below him to the Left side of* CREON. *She stands against
back of chair Right of the table)* What fun for you,
eh? To be able to laugh in the face of a king who has
all the power in the world; a man who has done his own
killing in his day; who has killed people just as pitiable
as you are—and who is still soft enough to go to all this
trouble in order to keep *you* from being killed. *(A moment, then)*
ANTIGONE. Now you are squeezing my arm too tight-
ly. It doesn't hurt any more.

(A pause. CREON *stares at her, then drops her arm. He
goes below the table to the chair at the Left end of
table, takes off his cape and places it on the chair.
ANTIGONE sits on chair Right of table. She looks
off toward the Right.)*

CREON. I shall save you yet. God knows, I have
things enough to do today without wasting my time
on an insect like you. *(He paces to upstage Center, then turns to her)* But urgent things can wait. I
am not going to let politics be the cause of your death.
*(He moves down to upper Right end of table. The
LIGHTING on the cyclorama gradually dims down to
a lower tone)* For it is a fact that this *whole* business
is nothing but politics: the mournful shade of Polynices, the decomposing corpse, the sentimental weeping
and the hysteria that you mistake for heroism, politics
—nothing but politics. *(He sits on upstage Right end
of table top)* Look here. I may be soft, but I'm fas-
tidious. I like things clean, shipshape, well scrubbed
Don't think that I am not just as offended as you are

by the thought of that—*meat*—rotting in the sun. (AN-
TIGONE *rises; stands with her back to him*) In the evening, when the breeze comes in off the sea, you can
smell it in the palace, and it nauseates me. But I refuse
even to shut my window. It is vile; and I can tell you
what I wouldn't tell anybody else: it's stupid, mon-
strously stupid. But the people of Thebes have got to
have their noses rubbed into it a little longer. My God!
If it was up to me, I should have had your brother
buried long ago as a mere matter of public hygiene.
But if the feather-headed rabble I govern are to understand what's what, that *stench* has got to fill the town
for a month!

ANTIGONE. *(Turns partly to him)* You are a *loath-
some* man!

CREON. I agree. My trade forces me to be. We could
argue whether I ought or ought not to follow my trade;
but once I take on the job, I must do it properly.

ANTIGONE. *(Turns fully to face him)* Why do you
do it at all?

CREON. My dear, I woke up one morning and found
myself king of Thebes. God knows, there were other
things I loved in life more than power.

ANTIGONE. Then you should have said no.

CREON. Yes— Yes, I could have said no. Only, I felt
that it would have been cowardly. I should have been
like a workman who turns down a job that has to be
done. So I said yes.

ANTIGONE. So much the worse for you, then. I didn't
say yes. I can say *no* to anything I think vile, and I
don't have to count the cost. But because you said *yes*
to your lust for power, all that you can do, for all of
your crown, your trappings, and your guards—all that
you can do is to have me killed.

CREON. Listen to me.

ANTIGONE. If I want to. I don't have to listen to you,
if I don't want to. There is nothing you can tell me
that I don't know. Whereas, there are a thousand things
I can tell you that you don't know. You stand there,
drinking in my words. Why is it that you don't call

your guards? I'll tell you why. You *want* to hear me out to the end and that's why.

CREON. You amuse me.

ANTIGONE. Oh, no, I don't. I frighten you. That is why you talk about saving me. Everything would be so .much easier if you had a docile, tongue-tied little Antigone living in the palace. But you are going to *have* to put me to death today, and you know it. And it frightens you.

CREON. Very well. I am afraid, then. Does that satisfy you? I am afraid that if you insist upon it, I shall have to have you killed. And I don't want to.

ANTIGONE. *I* don't have to do things that *I* think are wrong. If it comes to that, you didn't really want to leave my brother's body unburied, did you? Say it! Admit that you didn't.

CREON. I have said it already.

ANTIGONE. But you did it just the same. And now, though you don't want to, you are going to have me killed. And you call that being a king!

CREON. *(Stands up; spaces out his words)* Yes, I call *that* being a king.

ANTIGONE. Poor Creon! *My* nails are broken, *my* fingers are bleeding, *my* arms are covered with the welts left by the paws of your guards—but *I* am a queen!

CREON. Then why not have pity on me, and live? *(He gestures toward offstage up Right Center)* Isn't your brother's corpse, rotting beneath my windows, payment enough for peace and order in Thebes?

ANTIGONE. No. You said *yes*, and made yourself king. *Now* you will never stop paying.

CREON. But God in Heaven! Won't you *try* to understand me! I'm trying hard enough to understand *you!* There *had* to be one man who said yes. *(He moves a few steps upstage)* Somebody *had* to agree to captain the ship. She had sprung a hundred leaks; she was loaded to the waterline with crime, ignorance and poverty. The wheel was swinging with the wind. Every man-jack on board was about to drown—and only because the only thing they thought of was their own skins and their cheap little day-to-day traffic. Was that a time, do you think, for playing with words like yes and no? *(He moves down to Left of her)* Was that a time for a man to be weighing pros and cons, wondering if he wasn't going to pay too dearly, later on; wondering if he wasn't going to lose his life, or his family, or his touch with other men? *(He backs away a step Left)* You grab the wheel, you right the ship in the face of a mountain of water; you shout an order, and if *one* man refuses to obey, you shoot—straight into the mob. Into the mob, I say! A beast as nameless as the wave that crashes down upon your deck; as nameless as the whipping wind. The thing that drops when you shoot may be someone who poured you a drink the night before; but it has no name. And *you,* braced at the wheel, you have no name, either. Nothing has a name—except the ship, and the storm. *(A pause. He turns and moves to upper Right end of the table. Stands with his back to her)* Now do you understand?

ANTIGONE. I am not here to understand *these* things. I am here because I said *no* to you.

CREON. It is easy to say no.

ANTIGONE. Not always.

CREON. It is easy to say *no*. To say yes, you have to sweat and roll up your sleeves and plunge both hands into life up to the elbows. It is easy to say no, even if saying no means death. *(He turns to her)* All you have to do is to sit still and wait. Wait to go on living; wait to be killed. That is the coward's part. *No* is one of your man-made words. Can you imagine a world in which trees say *no* to the sap? In which beasts say *no* to hunger or to propagation? *(He moves to behind the table)* Animals are good, simple, tough. They move in droves, nudging one another onwards, all travelling the same road. Some of them keel over; but the rest go on; and no matter how many may fall by the wayside, there are always those few left who go on bringing their young into the world, travelling the same road with the same obstinate will, unchanged from those who went before.

ANTIGONE. *Animals!* Oh, what a *king you* could make, Creon, if only men were animals!

(A pause. CREON turns and looks at her.)

CREON. You despise me, don't you? (ANTIGONE *is silent.* CREON *goes on, as if to himself)* Strange. *(He sits on the stool behind table)* Again and again I have imagined this conversation with a pale young man I have never seen in the flesh. He would have come to assassinate me, and he would have failed. And I would be trying to find out from him why he wanted to kill me. But with all my logic and all my powers of debate, the only thing I could get out of him would be—that he despised me. *(He looks at her)* Who would have *thought* that that white-faced boy would turn out to be *you?* And that the debate would arise out of something so *meaningless*—as the burial of your brother? And yet, you must hear me out to the end. My part is not a heroic one, but I shall play my part: I shall have you put to death. But before I do, I want to make one last appeal. I want to be sure that *you* know what you are doing as well as I know what *I* am doing. Do you know what you are dying for, Antigone? *(He rises)* Do you know the sordid story to which you are going to sign your name in blood, for all time to come?

ANTIGONE. What story?

CREON. The story of Eteocles and Polynices, the story of your brothers. You think you know that story, but you don't. Nobody in Thebes knows that story but me. And today, I feel, that you have a right to know it, too. *(A pause as* ANTIGONE *moves to chair Right of table and sits)* It is *not* a pretty story. *(He turns, gets stool from behind the table and places it at the Right end of the table; between the table and the chair)* You shall see. *(He stands by the stool and looks at her for a moment)* Tell me, first. What do you remember about your brothers? They were older than you, so they must have looked down on you. And I imagine that they tormented you: pulled your pigtails, broke your dolls, whispered secrets to each other just to put you in a rage.

ANTIGONE. They were big and I was little.

CREON. And later on, when they came home wearing evening clothes, smoking cigarettes, strutting like men, they would take no notice of you and you thought they were wonderful.

ANTIGONE. They were boys and I was a girl.

CREON. You didn't know *why*, exactly, but you knew that they were making your mother unhappy. You saw her in tears over them; *(Goes above table to Left end of it)* and your father would fly into a rage because of them. You heard them come in, slamming doors, laughing noisily in the corridors—insolent, spineless, unruly, smelling of drink.

ANTIGONE. Once, it was very early and we had just got up. I saw them coming home, and hid behind a door. Polynices was pale and his eyes were shining. He was so handsome in his evening clothes. He saw me, and he said: "Here, this is for you," and he gave me a big paper flower that he had brought home from his night out.

CREON. And of course you still have that flower. Last night, before you crept out, you opened a drawer and looked at it for a time, to give yourself courage.

ANTIGONE. Who told you so?

CREON. *(Laughs)* Poor little Antigone! With her night-club flower. Do you know what your brother really was?

ANTIGONE. Whatever he was, I know that you will say vile things about him.

CREON. A cheap, idiotic bounder, that is what he was. A cruel, vicious little voluptuary. A little beast with just wit enough to drive a car faster and throw more money away than any of his pals. I was with your father one day when Polynices, who had lost a lot of money gambling, asked him to settle the debt; and when your father refused, the boy raised his hand against him and called him a vile name.

ANTIGONE. That's a lie!

CREON. He struck your father in the face with his fist. *(He pauses for a moment)* It was pitiful. Your father sat at his desk with his head in his hands. His nose was bleeding. He was weeping with anguish. And in a corner of your father's study, Polynices stood sneering and lighting a cigarette.

ANTIGONE. That's a lie.

(A pause. CREON crosses above table to the stool at Right and sits.)

CREON. When did you last *see* Polynices alive? When *you* were twelve years old. *That's* true, isn't it?

ANTIGONE. Yes, that's true.

CREON. Now you know why. Oedipus was too chicken-hearted to have the boy locked up. Polynices was allowed to go off and join the Argive army. And as soon as he reached Argos, the attempts upon your father's life began—upon the life of an old man who couldn't make up his mind to die, couldn't bear to be parted from his kingship. One after another, men slipped into Thebes from Argos for the purpose of assassinating him, and every killer that we caught, always ended by confessing *who* had put him up to it, *who* had paid him to try it. And Polynices wasn't the only one. *That* is really what I am trying to tell you. I want you to know what went on in the back room, in the *smelly kitchen* of politics; I want you to know what took place in the wings of this drama in which you are burning to play a part. (CREON *looks away from her*) Yesterday, I gave Eteocles a State funeral, with pomp and honors. Today, Eteocles is a saint and a hero in the eyes of all Thebes. The whole city turned out to bury him. The school children emptied their piggy-banks to buy wreaths for him. Old men, orating in quavering, hypocritical voices, glorified the virtues of the *great*-hearted brother, the devoted son, the loyal prince. I made a speech myself; and every temple priest was there with an appropriate show of sorrow and solemnity in his *stupid* face. And military honors were accorded the dead-hero. Well, what else could I have done? People had taken sides in the civil war. *Both* sides couldn't be wrong: that would have been too much. I couldn't have made them swallow the truth. *Two* gangsters was more of a—*luxury* than I could afford. *(He pauses for a moment)* And yet—*this* is the whole point of my story. *Eteocles,* that *virtuous* brother, was just as rotten as Polynices. That great-hearted son had done *his* best, too, to procure the assassination of his father. That *loyal* prince had also offered to sell out Thebes to the highest bidder. Funny, isn't it? Polynices lies rotting in the sun while Eteocles is given a hero's funeral and will be housed in a marble vault. Yet I have absolute proof that everything that Polynices did, Eteocles had plotted to do. They were a pair of blackguards—both intent in selling out Thebes, and both intent in selling out each other; and they died like the cheap gangsters they were, over a division of the spoils. But, as I told you a moment ago, I *had* to make a martyr of one of them. I sent out to the holocaust for their bodies: they were found clasped in one another's arms—for the first time in their lives, I imagine. Each had been spitted on the other's sword, and the Argive cavalry had trampled them down. There were—*mashed* —to a pulp, Antigone. I had the *prettier* of the two carcasses brought in, and gave it a State funeral; and I left the other to rot. I don't know which is which. And I assure you, I don't care.

(Long silence, neither looking at the other.)

ANTIGONE. *(In a mild voice)* Why do you tell me all this?

(A pause.)

CREON. You hold a treasure in your hands, Antigone

—life, I mean. And you were about to throw it away. Would it have been better to let you die a *victim* to that obscene story? *(He goes below table to chair Left end and picks up his cape from the chair; puts it on)* Antigone, go find Haemon and get married quickly. Be happy. Life is not what you think it is. Life is a *child* playing round your feet, a *tool* you hold firmly in your grip, a *bench* you sit down upon in the evening, in your garden. *(He goes above the table to upstage Left of her)* People will tell you that that's not life, that life is something else. They will tell you that because they need *your* strength and *your* fire, and they will want to make use of you. Don't *listen* to them. Believe me when I tell you—the only poor consolation that we have in our old age is to discover that what I have just said to you is true. Life is, perhaps, after all, nothing more than the happiness that you get out of it.

ANTIGONE. *(Murmurs, lost in thought)* Happiness—

CREON. *(Suddenly a little self-conscious)* Not much of a word, is it?

ANTIGONE. *(Quietly)* What kind of happiness do you foresee for me? Paint me the picture of your happy Antigone. What are the unimportant little sins that I shall have to commit before I am allowed to sink my teeth into life and tear happiness from it? Tell me: to whom shall I have to lie? upon whom shall I have to fawn? to whom must I sell myself? Whom do you want me to leave dying, while I turn away my eyes?

CREON. Antigone, be quiet. *(He sits on the stool.)*

ANTIGONE. Why do you ask me to be quiet when all I want is to know what I have to do to be happy? You tell me that life is so wonderful: I want to know what I must do in order to be able to say that myself.

CREON. Do you love Haemon?

ANTIGONE. Yes, I love Haemon. The Haemon I love is hard and young, and faithful and difficult to satisfy, the way I am. But if what I love in Haemon is to be worn away like a stone step by the tread of the thing you call life, the thing you call happiness; if Haemon reaches the point where he stops growing pale with fear when I grow pale, if he stops thinking that I have been killed in an accident when I am five minutes late, if he stops feeling alone on earth when I laugh and he doesn't know why—if he too has to *learn* to say *yes* to everything— *(She rises, turns and crosses to Right Center)* why no, then, no! I do *not* love Haemon!

CREON. *(Turns to face upstage)* You don't know what you are talking about!

ANTIGONE. *(Turns to him)* I *do* know what I am talking about! It is *you* who can't hear me! I am too far away from you now, talking to you from a kingdom you can't get into, *(She moves a step toward him)* with your preaching, and your politics, and your persuasive logic. I laugh at your smugness, Creon, thinking you could prove me wrong by telling me vile stories about my brothers or alter my purpose with your platitudes about happiness!

CREON. *(Looks at her)* It is *your* happiness, too, Antigone!

ANTIGONE. I *spit* on your idea of happiness! I *spit* on your idea of life—that life that must go on, come what may. You are all like dogs, that lick everything they smell. *You* with your promise of a humdrum happiness—provided a person doesn't ask too much of life. If life must be a thing of fear, and lying and compromise; if life cannot be free and incorruptible—then Creon, I choose death!

CREON. Scream on, daughter of Oedipus! *(He rises)* In your father's own voice!

ANTIGONE. *Yes!* In my father's own voice! We come of a tribe that asks questions; and we ask them remorselessly, to the bitter end. You have just told me the filthy reasons why *you* can't bury Polynices. *(She moves down to Right of him)* Now tell me why *I* can't bury him!

CREON. Because it is my order!

ANTIGONE. The order of a coward king who desecrates the dead!

CREON. *(Grasps her by her arms)* Be quiet! If you could see how *ugly* you are, shrieking those words!

ANTIGONE *(Pulls back from him, a few steps Right)*
Yes, I *am* ugly! Father was ugly, too. But father became beautiful. And do you know when? At the very end. When *all* his questions had been answered. (CREON *turns and moves away to above chair Left of table. Stands with his back to* ANTIGONE*)* When he could no longer doubt that he *had* killed his own father; that he *had* gone to bed with his own mother. When he was absolutely certain that he had to die if the plague was to be lifted from his people. *Then* he was at peace; *then* he could smile, almost; *then* he became beautiful— *(She moves around above him to up Left Center)* Whereas you! Look at yourself, Creon! That glint of fear and suspicion in the corner of your eyes—that crease in the corner of your power-loving mouth. Oh, you said the word a moment ago: the smelly kitchen of politics. *(She moves down to Left of him)* That's where you were fathered and whelped—*in a filthy kitchen!*

CREON. I *order* you to shut up! Do you hear me!

ANTIGONE. *You* order me? *Cook!* Do you really believe that *you* can give *me* orders?

CREON. *(Crosses behind table over toward the arch Right)* Antigone! The anteroom is full of people! Do you want them to hear you?

ANTIGONE. *(Turns toward him)* Open the doors! Let us make sure that they can hear me!

CREON. *(Turns and moves a few steps Left toward her)* By God! You shut up, I tell you!

ISMENE. *(Enters through arch Left and runs to behind the chair Left of table. Cries out, as she enters)* Antigone!

ANTIGONE. *(Below steps upstage Center. Turns to* ISMENE*)* You, too? What do *you* want?

ISMENE. Oh, forgive me, Antigone. I've come back. I'll go with you now.

ANTIGONE. *Where* will you go with me?

ISMENE. *(To* CREON*)* Creon! If you kill her, you'll have to kill me, too. I was with her. I helped her bury Polynices.

ANTIGONE. Oh, no, Ismene! You had your chance

to come with me in the black night, creeping on your hands and knees. You had your chance to claw up the earth with your nails and get yourself caught like a thief, as I did. And you refused it.

ISMENE. Not any more. If you die, I don't want to live. I'll do it alone tonight.

ANTIGONE. You hear that, Creon? *(She turns toward* CREON*)* The thing is catching! *(She moves down to behind the table)* Who knows but that others will catch the disease from me! What are you waiting for? Call in your guards! Come on, Creon! *(She moves toward him)* Show a little courage! It only hurts for a minute! Come on, *Cook!*

CREON. *(Turns toward arch Right and calls)* Guard!

*(*CREON *goes up on the top step, upstage Center. Instanly, the* FIRST GUARD *and* SECOND GUARD, *followed by the* THIRD GUARD, *enter through Right arch.)*

ANTIGONE. *(Moves to Right of* CREON; *in a great cry of relief)* At last, Creon!

CREON. *(To the* GUARDS*)* Take her away!

*(*CHORUS *enters through arch Left; stands below arch.* FIRST GUARD *crosses swiftly to the upstage side of* ANTIGONE; *the* SECOND GUARD *to her downstage side.* THIRD GUARD *remains in front of arch Right. The* TWO GUARDS *grasp* ANTIGONE *by her arms, turn her and hustle her toward the arch Right and exit, followed by the* THIRD GUARD.*)*

ISMENE. *(Takes a few steps toward* CREON*)* Oh, no! Creon! (*ISMENE *turns and runs out through arch Left.)*

(A pause as CREON *moves slowly down to behind table.)*

CHORUS. *(Moves Left a few steps to behind chair Left of the table)* You are out of your mind, Creon. What have you done?

CREON. *(With his back to* CHORUS; *not looking at him)* She had to die.

CHORUS. You must not let Antigone die. We shall carry the scar of her death for centuries.

CREON. No man on earth was strong enough to dissuade her. Polynices was a mere pretext.

CHORUS. That is not the truth, Creon—and you know it.

CREON. What do you want me to do for her? Condemn her to live?

(He turns, goes up to top step upstage Center and is about to exit when HAEMON *enters through arch Right and crosses over to Right of* CREON.)

HAEMON. *Father!*

CREON. *(Comes down to the second step)* Forget Antigone, Haemon. Forget her, my dearest boy.

HAEMON. How can you talk like that?

CREON. I did everything I could to save her, Haemon. I used every argument. I swear I did. The girl doesn't love you. She could have gone on living for you; but she refused. She *wanted* it this way: she *wanted* to die.

HAEMON. Father! They are dragging Antigone away! You've got to stop them!

(The LIGHTING dims down to a lower level.)

CREON. *(Moves away to above Left end of the table)* I can't stop them. It's too late. Antigone has spoken. I cannot save her now.

HAEMON. You must!

CREON. I cannot.

HAEMON. Recall your edict. Bury Polynices.

CREON. Too late. The law must be obeyed. I can do nothing.

HAEMON. But, Father, *you* are master in Thebes!

CREON. I am master *under* the law. Not *above* the law.

HAEMON. But you made that law yourself, and what you ordained, you can repeal. *(He moves down to Right of* CREON*)* You cannot let Antigone be taken from me.

CREON. I cannot do anything else, my boy. She must die and you must live.

HAEMON. *Live!* For what? A life without Antigone? A life in which I am to go on admiring you as you busy yourself about your kingdom; go on admiring you as you make your persuasive speeches and strike your attitudes? Not without Antigone. I love Antigone. She never struck a pose and waited for me to admire her Mirrors meant nothing to her. She never looked at herself. She looked at *me,* and expected me to be somebody. And I was—when I was with her. Do you think I am not going after her? I will not live without Antigone!

CREON. Haemon—you will have to resign yourself to life without Antigone. Sooner or later there comes a day of sorrow in each man's life when he must cease to be a child and take up the burden of being a man. That day has come for you.

HAEMON. That giant strength, that courage. That massive god who used to pick me up in his arms and shelter me from shadows and monsters—was that *you,* Father? Was it of *you* I stood in awe? Was that man *you?*

(The LIGHTING begins dimming to a lower level.)

CREON. Yes, Haemon, that was me.

HAEMON. You are *not* that man today. For if you were, you'd know that your enemies were abroad in every street. You'd know that the people revere those gods that you despise. You cannot put Antigone to death. She will not have been dead an hour, before shame will sit on every Theban forehead and horror will fill every Theban heart. Already the people curse you because you do not bury Polynices. If you kill Antigone, they will *hate* you!

CREON. *Silence!* That edict stands!

(HAEMON *stares at* CREON *for a moment, then turns
and quickly goes out through Right arch. The
LIGHTING dims down even lower. A pause, as*
CREON *moves to above Right end of the table.*)

CHORUS. Creon, the gods have a way of punishing
injustice.

CREON. *(Facing toward Right arch; contemptuously)*
The *gods!*

CHORUS. Creon, that boy is wounded to death.

CREON. *(Turns to* CHORUS*)* We are *all* wounded to
death.

(FIRST GUARD *rushes in hurriedly through the Right
arch and crosses to upstage Right Center.* AN-
TIGONE *runs in behind him and lurches up against
the upstage portal of the arch, breathless and dis-
hevelled. Then the* SECOND *and* THIRD GUARDS
*follow in. They both literally hurl themselves upon
her, grasping her arms roughly and with force.
They drag her over to Right Center, the* SECOND
GUARD *stands above her, the* THIRD GUARD *below
her.*)

FIRST GUARD. Chief, the people are crowding into
the palace!

ANTIGONE. Creon! I don't want to hear them howl
anymore! You are going to kill me: let that be enough.
I want to be alone until it is over.

CREON. *(To the* TWO GUARDS *holding* ANTIGONE*)*
Empty the palace! Guards at the gates!

(CREON *goes quickly toward the arch Right and exits.
The* TWO GUARDS *release their hold on* ANTIGONE
and exit behind CREON. *The* CHORUS *turns and
goes out through arch Left. The LIGHTING
quickly dims so that only the area around the table
is lighted. The cyclorama is covered with a dark
blue color. The scene is intended to suggest a
prison cell, filled with shadows and dimly lit.* AN-

*TIGONE moves to the chair at Right end of table
and sits. The FIRST GUARD stands upstage Right
Center watching her. After she sits, he begins pac-
ing slowly up and down stage Right. A pause.)*

ANTIGONE. *(Turns and looks at the GUARD)* It's you,
is it?

GUARD. *(Halts downstage Right Center; looks at
her)* What do you mean?

ANTIGONE. The last human face that I shall see. *(A
pause. He then walks upstage and slowly crosses behind
the table to up Left Center)* Was it you that arrested
me this morning?

GUARD. Yeah, that was me.

ANTIGONE. You hurt me. There was no need for
you to hurt me. Did I act as if I were trying to escape?

GUARD. Come on now, Miss. It was my business to
arrest you! I did it.

*(A pause. He paces behind table to upstage Right Cen-
ter. Only the sound of his boots is heard.)*

ANTIGONE. How old are you?

GUARD. Thirty-nine. *(He turns and paces over to up
Left Center.)*

ANTIGONE. Have you any children?

GUARD. Yeah. Two.

ANTIGONE. Do you love your children?

GUARD. What's that got to do with you?

*(A pause. He walks upstage Left, then turns and walks
downstage Left.)*

ANTIGONE. How long have you been in the Guards?

GUARD. *(Moves to below and behind chair Left)*
Since the war, I was in the army. Sergeant. Then I
joined the Guards. But when they make you a guard,
you lose your stripes.

ANTIGONE. *(Murmurs)* I see.

GUARD. *(Paces upstage)* Yeah. Of course, if you're

a guard, everybody knows you're something special; they know you're an old non-com. *(He moves to Left end of the table)* Take pay, for instance. When you're a guard you get your pay, and on top of that you get six months extra pay, to make sure you don't lose anything by not being a sergeant any more.

ANTIGONE. *(Barely audible)* I see.

GUARD. *(Moves to Right end of table and sits on it)* That's what I'm telling you. That's why sergeants, now, they don't like guards. Maybe you noticed they try to make out they're better than us? Promotion, that's what it is. In the army, anybody can get promoted. Take a look around your own boy-friends. All you need is good conduct. Now in the Guards, it's slow, and you have to know your business—like how to make out a report and the like of that. But when you're a non-com in the guards, you've got something that even a sergeant-major ain't got. For instance—

ANTIGONE. *(Breaking him off)* Listen.

GUARD. Yes, Miss.

ANTIGONE. I'm going to die soon.

GUARD. *(The GUARD looks at her for a moment, stands up and moves away to behind chair Left of table)* For instance, people have a lot of respect for guards, they have. A guard may be a soldier, but he's kind of in the civil service, too.

ANTIGONE. Do you think it hurts to die?

GUARD. How would I know? Of course, if somebody sticks a sabre in your guts and turns it round, it hurts.

ANTIGONE. How are they going to put me to death?

GUARD. *(Moves to upper Left end of the table)* Well, I'll tell you. I heard the proclamation, all right. There isn't much that gets away from me. It seems that they don't want to— Wait a minute. How did that go now? *(He stares into space and recites from memory)* "In order that our fair city shall not be pol-!uted with her sinful blood, she shall be im-mured—immured." *(He looks at her)* That means, they shove you in a cave and wall up the cave.

ANTIGONE. *(Sits up, erect) Alive?*

GUARD. Yes— *(He looks away from her.)*

ANTIGONE. *(Murmurs as she slumps)* O tomb! O bridal bed! Alone!

GUARD. Yep! Outside the southeast gate of the town. In the Caves of Hades. In broad daylight. *(He moves around to behind the Left chair)* Some detail, eh, for them that's on the job? First they thought maybe it was a job for the army. Now it looks like it's going to be the Guards. There's an outfit for you! Nothing the Guards can't do. No wonder the army's jealous.

ANTIGONE. A pair of animals.

GUARD. *(Looks at her, puzzled)* What do you mean, a pair of animals?

ANTIGONE. When the winds blow cold, all they need to do is to press close against one another. I am all alone.

GUARD. *(Moves to upper end of table, and bends over toward her)* Say, is there anything you want? I can send out for it, you know.

ANTIGONE. You are very kind. *(A pause. Then AN- TIGONE looks up at the GUARD)* Yes, there is something I want. I want you to give someone a letter from me, when I am dead.

GUARD. How's that again? A *letter?*

ANTIGONE. Yes, I want to write a letter; and I want you to give it to someone for me.

GUARD. *(Straightens up)* Hey, wait a minute. Take it easy. It's as much as my job is worth to go handing out letters from prisoners.

ANTIGONE. *(Removes a ring from her finger and holds it out toward him)* I'll give you this ring if you will do it.

GUARD. *(He takes the ring from her, examines it, then shakes his head)* Uh-uh. No can do. Suppose they go through my pockets. I might get six months for a thing like that— *(He stares at the ring, then glances off Right to make sure that he is not being watched; then he sits on the stool, bends over toward her)* Lis- ten, tell you what I'll do. You tell me what you want to say, and I'll write it down in my book. Then afterwards, I'll tear out the pages and give them to the party, see? If it's in my handwriting, it's all right.

ANTIGONE. *(Winces)* In *your* handwriting? *(She shudders slightly)* Oh, the poor darling! In *your* handwriting.

GUARD. *(Stands up; offers back the ring)* O.K. It's no skin off my nose.

ANTIGONE. *(Quickly)* No, keep it, but be quick about it. Time is getting short. Where is your notebook? *(The GUARD pockets the ring, takes his notebook and pencil from his pocket, sits on the stool beside her, and rests the notebook on his knee, licks his pencil)* Ready? *(He nods)* Write, now. "My darling—"

GUARD. *(Writes as he mutters)* The boy-friend, eh?

ANTIGONE. "My darling. I had to die, and perhaps you will not love me any more—"

GUARD. *(Mutters as he writes)* "—love me any more."

ANTIGONE. "Perhaps you think it would have been simple to accept life—"

GUARD. *(Repeats as he writes)* "—to accept life—"

ANTIGONE. "But it was not for myself. And now, it's all—so dreadful here alone. I am afraid— *(She glances wildly about)* And those shadows—"

GUARD. *(Looks at her)* Hey, take it easy! How fast do you think I can write?

ANTIGONE. *(In despair. Takes hold of herself)* Where are you?

GUARD. *(Reads from his notebook)* "—dreadful here alone. I am afraid—"

ANTIGONE. No. Scratch that out. Nobody must know that. They have no right to know. It's as if they saw me naked and touched me, after I am dead. Scratch that out. Just write: "Forgive me."

GUARD. *(Looks at her)* I scratch out everything you said there at the end, and I put down, "Forgive me?"

ANTIGONE. Yes. "Forgive me, my darling. You would all have been so happy if it hadn't been for Antigone. I love you." *(She murmurs, as GUARD writes)* No, it wasn't for myself.

GUARD. *(Finishes the letter)* "—been for Antigone. I love you." *(He looks at her)* Is that all?

ANTIGONE. That's all.

GUARD. *(Straightens up)* You know—that's a funny kind of letter—

ANTIGONE. I know.

GUARD. Now who is it to?

(There is a sudden, sharp roll of drums sounding from offstage Right and continuing until after the exit of ANTIGONE and the three GUARDS. The SECOND and THIRD GUARDS enter quickly through the Right arch. Both ANTIGONE and the FIRST GUARD rise hurriedly at the sound of the drums.)

ANTIGONE. *(Turns to FIRST GUARD, pleadingly)* But I haven't finished yet—

FIRST GUARD. *(Pockets his notebook and pencil; shouts at her)* Shut up!

(The Two GUARDS advance toward ANTIGONE, grasp her arms and roughly hustle her toward the arch Right and out The FIRST GUARD follows them. As they exit, the LIGHTS dim out quickly, leaving only the cyclorama dimly lighted. The DRUM ROLL rises in a sharp crescendo and ends on a loud note. A pause. The DRUM is heard as from a distance, striking a measured beat, five times. After the fifth beat of the drum, the CHORUS appears through the vent in cyclorama upstage Center and stands on the top step there. A single LIGHT dims up to cover the CHORUS.)

CHORUS. It is over for Antigone. And now it is Creon's turn.

(The other LIGHTS on the stage dim up to suggest late afternoon.)

MESSENGER. *(The MESSENGER runs in through the*

*Right arch, and stands in front of the upstage portal
of the arch, breathless and exhausted)* The Queen—
the Queen—! *(He crosses toward the* CHORUS*)* Where
is the Queen?

CHORUS. *(Turns toward the* MESSENGER*)* What do
you want with the Queen? What have you to tell the
Queen?

MESSENGER. *(Goes up the steps, leans against the*
CHORUS *for support, still gasping for breath)* News to
break her heart. Antigone had been thrust into the cave.
They hadn't finished heaving the last blocks of stone
into place, when Creon and the rest heard a sudden
moaning from the tomb. A hush fell over us all, for it
was not the voice of Antigone. It was Haemon's voice
that came forth from the tomb. Everybody looked at
Creon; and he howled like a man demented: "Take
away the stones! Take away the stones!" The slaves
leapt at the wall of stones, and Creon worked with
them, sweating and tearing at the blocks with bleeding
hands. Finally a narrow opening was forced, and into
it slipped the smallest guard. Antigone had hanged herself by the cord of her robe, by the red and golden
twisted cord of her robe. The cord was round her neck
like a child's collar. Haemon was on his knees, holding
her in his arms and moaning, his face buried in her
robe. More stones were removed, and Creon went into
the tomb. He tried to raise Haemon to his feet. I could
hear him begging Haemon to rise to his feet. Haemon
was deaf to his father's voice; till suddenly he stood up
of his own accord, his eyes dark and burning. Anguish
was in his face. He stared at his father. Then suddenly
he struck him—hard in the face, then he pulled out a
knife and lunged at his father. Creon leapt out of
range. Haemon went on staring at him, his eyes full of
contempt—a glance that Creon couldn't escape. The
king stood trembling at the far corner of the tomb,
and Haemon went on staring. Then, without a word,
he stabbed himself and lay down beside Antigone,
(CREON and his PAGE *enter through arch Right and
cross slowly to Right Center, the* PAGE *on* CREON'S

downstage side) embracing her in a great pool of **blood.**
(The MESSENGER *turns and looks at* CREON, *then goes through vent in curtain upstage Center.)*

(A pause.)

CREON. I have had them laid out side by side. They are together at last, and at peace. Two lovers on the morrow of their bridal. Their work is done.

CHORUS. *(With a sudden gesture of recollection)* But not *yours,* Creon. *(He comes down off steps to behind Center of the table)* You have still one thing to learn. Eurydice, the queen, your wife—

CREON. A good woman.

CHORUS. When the queen was told of her son's death, she waited carefully until she had finished her row, then put down her knitting calmly—as she did everything. She went up to her room and there, Creon, she cut her throat. She is laid out now exactly where you went to her one night when she was still a maiden. Her smile is still the same; one might think she was asleep.

CREON. She, too. They are all asleep. *(A pause. Then, in a dull voice)* It must be good to sleep.

CHORUS. Tomorrow they will sleep sweetly in the earth, Creon. And you will bury them. You who would not bury Polynices today will bury Eurydice and Haemon tomorrow. And Antigone, too. The gods take a hand in every game, Creon. Even in politics.

CREON. The task is there to be done. They say it's dirty work. But if I didn't do it, who would?

CHORUS. Why must dirty work be done? *(A pause)* And now you are alone, Creon. *(He turns and faces away from* CREON.*)*

CREON. Yes, all alone. *(He crosses slowly up to top step, upstage Center. A pause, then the CLOCK strikes five)* What time is it?

PAGE. *(Moves up to below and Right of* CREON*)* Five o'clock, Sir.

CREON. What have we on today at five o'clock?

PAGE. Cabinet meeting, Sir.

CREON. Cabinet meeting. Then we had better get along to it.

(PAGE *goes up the steps to Right of* CREON. *They exit through vent in cyclorama upstage Center. A pause. Then* CHORUS *moves down to below Left end of table.)*

CHORUS. And there we are. All those who were meant to die, have died: those who believed one thing, those who believed the contrary thing, and even those who believed nothing at all, yet were caught up in the web without knowing why. All dead: useless, rotting. Creon was the most rational, the most persuasive of tyrants. But like all tyrants, he refused to distinguish between the things that are Caesar's and the things that are God's. Now and again—in the three thousand years since the first Antigone—other Antigones have arisen like a clarion call to remind men of this distinction. Their cause is always the same—a passionate belief that moral law exists, and a passionate regard for the sanctity of human dignity. Well, Antigone is calm tonight. She has played her part. (*The* THREE GUARDS *enter through arch Right and resume their former places on the steps. They begin playing a game of cards*) A great wave of unrest now settles down upon Thebes, upon the empty palace, upon Creon, who can now begin to long for his own death. Only the Guards are left, and none of this matters to them. It's no skin off their noses. They go on playing cards.

(*The Curtain falls. The* CHORUS *goes to arch Left and exits.)*

END

ANTIGONE

PROPERTY PLOT

On Stage—
    All-over gray colored ground cloth
    Gray painted table
    2 gray painted matching side chairs
    1 gray painted stool
        (Note: Seats and backs upholstered in gray
           material)

Off Stage—
    Pair of practical handcuffs (with lock "tricked")
        Right
    Notebook and small stub pencil for FIRST GUARD
    Handcuff key for FIRST GUARD
    Deck of playing cards for FIRST GUARD
    Knitting and needles for EURYDICE
    Gold ring for ANTIGONE
    Pair of sandals for ANTIGONE
    Tympanni drum and sticks
    Black cape for CREON
    Cigarette case and lighter for CHORUS

Off Left—
    Shawl and apron for NURSE
    Set of chimes and drum stick

ANTIGONE

WARDROBE

ANTIGONE:
    Costume (green dress with red and gold cord
        sash)

ISMENE:
    Costume
    Shoes

EURYDICE:
    Costume
    Shoes

NURSE:
    Costume
    Apron
    Shawl
    Shoes

CREON:
    Evening clothes ("Tails")
    Black cape

CHORUS: Evening clothes ("Tails")

HAEMON: Evening clothes ("Tails")

FIRST GUARD:
    Dinner jacket
    Navy blue trench coat (no hat)

SECOND GUARD:
    Dinner jacket
    Navy blue trench coat
    Hat

THIRD GUARD:
    Dinner jacket
    Navy blue trench coat
    Hat

73

MESSENGER:
Dinner jacket
Tan trench coat
No hat

PAGE:
Gray striped long trousers
Oxford gray Eton jacket and vest
Eton collar and black tie
Black oxford shoes

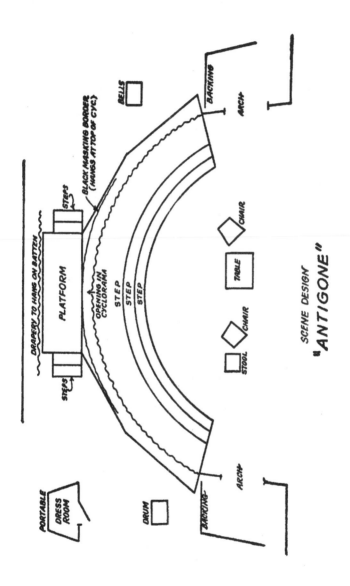

SCENE DESIGN

"ANTIGONE"